The day Ruth Maguire encounters the wet man on the lonely Wrack Road seems no different to any other, but their meeting on bleak Dooney Headland, where Ruth lives with her mother and brother and little sister, has terrifying consequences. Ruth's ordeal, trapped in her own home with the lives of James and little Katya at stake, builds to a nightmare intensity against a background of grey slab rocks and the glittering sea, in a remote place which is a little world of its own.

Catherine Sefton has written a taunt and thrilling novel which confronts the reality of a young girl trapped in a threatening situation where there is no easy way out.

Catherine Sefton is the pseudonym of Martin Waddell, a distinguished writer for children of all ages. Winner of the 1988 Smarties Award, the 1989 Kurt Maschler Award and the 1986 Other Award, he was also shortlisted for the *Young Observer* Teenage Fiction Prize and runner up for The *Guardian* Children's Fiction Award. He lives in Newcastle, Co. Down with his wife and three sons.

By the same author

BERTIE BOGGIN AND THE GHOST AGAIN!
THE GHOST AND BERTIE BOGGIN
IN A BLUE VELVET DRESS

Along A
Lonely
Road

Catherine Sefton

PUFFIN BOOKS

PUFFIN BOOKS

Published by the Penguin Group
Penguin Books Ltd, 27 Wrights Lane, London W8 5TZ, England
Penguin Books USA Inc., 375 Hudson Street, New York, New York 10014, USA
Penguin Books Australia Ltd, Ringwood, Victoria, Australia
Penguin Books Canada Ltd, 10 Alcorn Avenue, Toronto, Ontario, Canada M4V 3B2
Penguin Books (NZ) Ltd, 182–190 Wairau Road, Auckland 10, New Zealand

Penguin Books Ltd, Registered Offices: Harmondsworth, Middlesex, England

First published by Hamish Hamilton 1991
Published in Puffin Books 1993
1 3 5 7 9 10 8 6 4 2

Printed in England by Clays Ltd, St Ives plc
Filmset in Baskerville

'See this?' he said.

It was a gun.

'It goes off if you pull the trigger,' he said.

'Do you understand me, Ruth?'

'Yes.'

'Your mother has two small children in there,' he said. 'You wouldn't want anything to happen to them, would you?'

'No.'

'Well then, be a good girl and behave yourself,' he said.

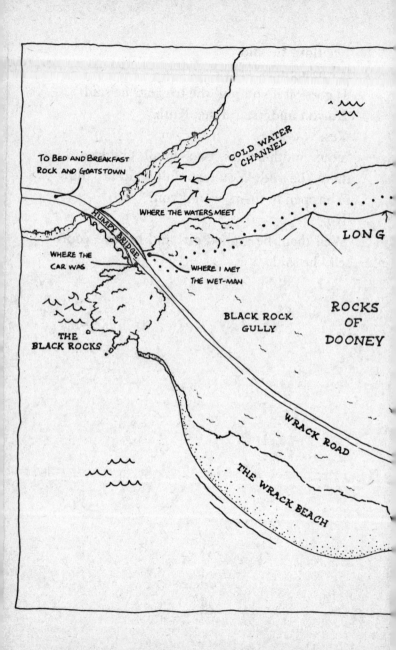

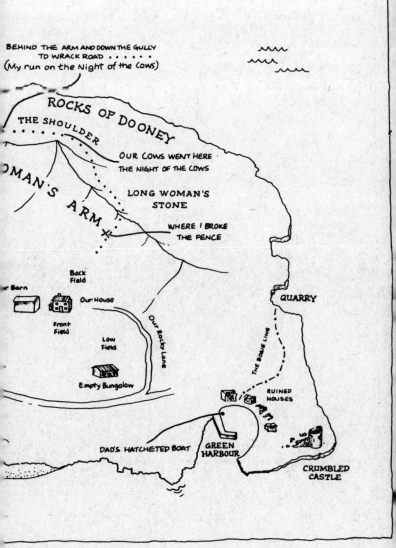

BEHIND THE ARM AND DOWN THE GULLY
TO WRACK ROAD • • • • • •
(My run on the Night of the Cows)

ROCKS OF DOONEY

THE SHOULDER
• • • •

OUR COWS WENT HERE •
THE NIGHT OF THE COWS

OMAN'S ARM

LONG WOMAN'S
STONE

WHERE I BROKE
THE FENCE

Back
Field

r Barn

Our House

Front
Field

Low
Field

Our Rocky Lane

Empty Bungalow

QUARRY

THE Bone LINE

RUINED
HOUSES

DAD'S HATCHETED BOAT

GREEN
HARBOUR

CRUMBLED
CASTLE

Chapter 1

'You'll take the eggs into Mrs Hannigan's, Ruth,' my mother said, firmly.

'It's not me!' I said. 'It is down to James!'

'I can't send the child,' she said. 'Not a cold morning like that, on his own.'

'There is more of me to freeze!' I muttered but she didn't heed me.

I was mad!

She wasn't going to argue about it.

I was for the lonely Wrack Road through the rocks of Dooney on my old bone-shaking bicycle, all the way in off the headland and all the way out again, and never mind the bitter wind that would cut swathes out of me on the humpy bridge.

I got the egg box loaded on the bike, and wrapped myself up in all I could find. On my way out, wrapped up like a Polar explorer, I looked into the kitchen, and there was James, in his pyjamas with his red head down in his detective book, curled up on the sofa in front of the range like a cosy kitten.

'You are a mean wee devil, James Maguire!' I told him sourly. 'You'd get out of anything that didn't suit you.'

'It's only Hannigan's and back,' he said. 'And you're bigger than me and you have the bike. I have no bike and I'd have to walk it.'

'It's not my bike,' I said. 'It is supposed to be a family bike, for getting us in and out.' It is an old bone-shaker out of the ark anyway, and no bike to be proud of.

'I don't fit it!' James said, snuggling down on the sofa. 'I have short legs. You have the legs of a young giraffe!'

'Are you calling me a giraffe?' I asked, advancing on him.

'Ruth! Ruth! Are you not gone yet?' my mum called down the stairs. 'Get dressed and go!'.

'See you James Maguire?' I said, heading for the door. 'You are as good as dead when I get back!'

I could count on the wind to blow me in to Goatstown, that was one consolation, but I knew it would be in my face all the way back to Dooney which is no joke. The wind has Dooney headland scarred down to the dark rock. There are only the few fields round our house in the shelter of the Long Woman's Arm that would even feed a beast. The rest of the headland is fit for nothing but the gulls and foxes and Pearce McRobert's goat that he used to keep there till it died. There was no replacement for the goat when the cold got it.

'Will you bring me sweeties?' Katya asked, when I was going out the porch.

'Have you any money?' I said.

'No, I have not,' Katya said.

'Did you look in your purse?' I said.

She's smart enough for a four-year-old. I know her tricks. We got her purse from under the big chair and she looked in it, but right enough there was no money.

'Will you get me sweeties just the same?' she said, wheedling me.

'Well, I might and I might not,' I said.

'Ruth! Will you get going *now*!' my mum bawled down the stairs.

'Bye-bye!' Katya said.

'Bye-bye you!' I said, grumpy enough although not with her, for it wasn't her fault, and off I went.

The wind was cutting off the Shoulder when I was wheeling the bike down our Rocky Lane to the Wrack Road, and my nose was blue before I could mount her. Even then it was a humpy ride, for our lonely old road is hardly a road at all these days, with only our own van and the postman along it. The farmers used to use it for drawing seaweed from the Wrack Beach at Dooney to lay on the land as a kind of fertilizer. That stuff all comes out of plastic bags now, so the road is no use, except for our comings and goings. Our old headland at Dooney is the end of the world, with the sea on three sides of it breaking in the bays, and the rush and thunder of the Cold Water Estuary between us and the mainland, and only the humpy bridge to keep us connected at all. There would never have been a humpy bridge if it hadn't been for the Famine Relief in the 1840s, and with the battering of the arches when the tide is up the estuary there may soon be no bridge at all, for you can see she is coming apart. I don't suppose the rest of the world would miss it if she went, for we are the only ones left out on Dooney headland since the quarrymen went at the end of the war, but if the bridge ever goes down the Cold Water we'll be in a mess.

All this is my way of telling how-I-met-the-wet-man. I suppose in a way it is just as well it was me that went with the eggs, and not James. There is no knowing what James' nosiness might have let him in for. I suppose he would have been all right. With his head full of his old stories he'd have come home telling the tale, but I think we would have paid no heed to him. It is all *Secret Seven* and *Five Find-Outers* with him, Alfred Hitchcock, adventures and detective stuff, and his mouth is bigger than his mind. We wouldn't have listened to him, but he might have got himself into trouble just the same.

Anyway, I met the wet-man by the humpy bridge, not James.

You'll understand that anyone on our road is a novelty, especially in winter. There is no call for anybody to be using it, but us. But there he was, bending into the rain, wet and dripping in hiker stuff, all muffled up to meet the blast, which was blowing me down the bumpy road, but blowing hard in his face.

'Hello there!' he said, waving an arm at me to stop, so I did a slither and stopped, which is no easy thing when you have claw brakes with the rubbers gone.

He was a big man, a stranger to me, with a raw nose poking out of his scarf and a pair of gold glasses held with a tape round the side of his head.

'It's a damp day for a hike!' I told him, civil enough, but no more than civil. How else would I be to a stranger on our road?

'Would I be right for the castle?' he said.

'Well, there is no castle!' I said.

'What's that?' he said, leaning into the wind, with his face turned towards me away from it.

'The bits that are left are just bits,' I said. 'But you are right for it if you want to go there.' I was wondering if he was in his right mind, walking our lonely old Wrack Road to the castle on a day like that.

'Do you *live* out there?' he said, plainly taken with the thought.

'Aye,' I said.

'I thought no one lived at Dooney any more,' he said.

'Well, we do,' I said.

'How long have you lived here?' he asked, getting nosey.

'Long enough,' I said. 'Now if you'll pardon me I'll be getting on!'

He must have sensed by the cut of me that I wasn't one for answering questions with the wind blowing a gale up my back.

'You were very good to help me,' he said, and tugged up his scarf round his cheeks and trudged on the way I had come.

That was it.

That was the time I met the wet-man.

From all that passed between us there was nothing in our meeting to make the moment pass-remarkable, although if I'd known then what I know now I might have thought differently.

As it was I got into Goatstown and did the business with the eggs and got the month's money off Mrs Hannigan, which was no small wonder, and then I did myself a good turn by hitching a lift back, bike and all, on Benjy Murnaghan's trailer clutching Katya's sweetie bag. The cows in our fields are Murnaghan's, and we have an arrangement for looking after them, so the conversation was all heifers and bullocks and I never thought to mention the mad wet-man on the road to him. Benjy let me off by the humpy bridge and I trudged over with the spray coming round me and then off up the Wrack Road between the grey slab boulders, pushing the bike though with a good mind to dump her in the Black Rocks, for there was no way I could ride. The old gully on the Black Rocks was going a dinger, a real waterfall.

I half thought I might meet the wet-man coming back, but I didn't. He hadn't called up at the house either, which he might have, seeing it is the only lived-in house around. I supposed at the time that he might have tried McRobert's old empty bungalow, two fields below us, just above Green Harbour, but I supposed he'd drawn a blank there and couldn't face the haul up our Rocky Lane, with the water trickling down it like a stream.

That's what I supposed.

I'd suppose it different now.

It wasn't our house or what's left of Corr's crumbly castle at the Long Woman's Arm he was after, but something entirely different.

I must have been a shock to him! He could have come in a car and done his business, but I suppose he was afraid someone might spot it, or else he was safeguarding his springs ... our Wrack Road is no place for fancy cars.

Anyway, he walked out to Dooney in the rain and the wind, and I can only suppose he walked in again, but he made sure no one else saw him, for no one did, though I've asked about Goatstown since.

Who would have been likely to see him anyway? Only us, or the Murnaghans if they happened to be out asking about their cattle, or the Coadys at their cottage on the Goatstown Road.

He would have known that.

After all, that was the whole point of it.

Chapter 2

What happened next?

Nothing happened next, but this isn't a nothing-happened-next story. When things started to happen they happened all at once, one after the other, so fast that I couldn't get my head turned to think about them, but back *then* . . . nothing. Just cold old February days, after I met the wet-man.

March. The IRA blew up the Creamery in Cross. Joe Milligan from Goatstown got the blast across the road, and ended up with his car through the window of Camerons' Butchers. The wet-man was nothing to do with the IRA, that is just what happened in March.

April. My dad was back for my fourteenth birthday and Father Dillon died and got buried in Cross. The school trip down to Dublin got cancelled over him dying. James went to Belfast for a football match with my dad and he was sick in the van coming back. I got lumbered with cleaning it up, which is the way it goes when you are the big child at home, in a house with two small ones.

May. My father was off to England again in the van to make us a bit of money. It rained a lot.

June. My mother was into Caffertys' just outside Cross for barbed wire for the cattle and Mrs Cafferty told her there had been someone in asking about us, but no word of who it was. Mrs Cafferty never let on that she spoke a word about us, but I would take that with a pinch of salt. Anyway, by that time they must have had us figured out.

July. There was a pack of French students camping by the Quarry, but I don't think they had anything to do with anything, beyond dumping their litter in the old buildings at Green Harbour, which we could have done without.

It was August it happened in.

James and I had Katya up by the Long Woman's Stone, which is just our side of the Shoulder. It is supposed to be her grave, if there ever was a Long Woman. There must have been a lot of Long Women in Ireland, for their graves are all over the place.

The cattle had the fence down, and James was

doing the poles and I was doing the barbed wire, for fear he would cut himself and bleed to death after doing it. Katya was sitting on the stone making daisy-chains.

'There's someone coming on the Wrack Road,' Katya said.

We looked, and there was. A wee van.

'It will be old Murnaghan,' James said.

'I think not!' I said. 'For this is Wednesday, and he is to come to settle our money at the end of the week, and he never comes early when it is pay week.'

'Well, it might be.'

'It'll be B&B,' I said, losing interest.

Time was, before we were ever on the headland, that the people in the empty bungalow, the McRoberts, did B&B for city people that were touring round. They had a sign painted on the rocks before the turn off for the humpy bridge, and the Bed and Breakfasters came out and stayed in their back room, the one without the damp in the wall. Pearce McRobert let on they made a fortune at it. Only it can't have been much of a fortune because they sold up and moved into Goatstown, first chance they got. They took the B&B Vacancies sign off the hook outside their house with them, but they never did anything about the sign painted on the rocks, and for a while after we came lost Bed and Breakfasters came out and tried to talk Mum into taking them till she got mad and bought whitewash and Dad did the rock sign all over. That stopped it, but the odd stray still turns up.

So that is what we thought the someone was.

We thought so little of it that we didn't even go down to the house to see.

If a fence is down it needs seeing to before anything else, and that is what we were out to do. Anyway, very few of the B&B strays can face bringing their cars up our lane, for the tarmac ends at the bungalow below, and our Rocky Lane is still a long haul after that.

That's as maybe.

When we got back to the house, there was the van in the yard.

We were on our way over our old crumbly wall when I looked up, and saw my mother at the back window.

She had a fierce look on.

Her cheeks were fiery red, and her red hair was rumpled.

She saw me at the moment I saw her, and she made a quick move with her hand, as if to say get-them-out-of-the-way, meaning James and Katya.

Well, I didn't know what was up, but by the same token I knew something was.

'Hold on, James!' I said, turning round on him as he was coming off the wall. 'Did you have Dad's red pliers?'

'We never had them with us,' James said.

'Well, we did,' I said, congratulating myself on being quick off the mark. 'I'm sure we did. And it was you that had them in the bag, and Mum'll be mad if they are left out in the field to rust.'

We're not supposed to use Dad's big cutting pliers, particularly James, who is always letting on that he is a workman like my father.

'You're to go and get them,' I said. 'Go on now, for if anything happens to them there'll be a row.'

'They won't be there!' he said.

'Well, if they aren't we'll know they aren't, won't we?' I said.

I didn't want him to argue, and I think maybe he half realized there was more to it, for he gave me a queer look, and then off he went.

'We'll just have a look-see in the barn, Katya,'
I said.

'What for?' she said.

'I don't know,' I said. 'Fairies!'

'There isn't any fairies,' she said. 'You know
there isn't. There is only fairies in stories.'

'Well, there might be,' I said. 'You never know
with stories what is true and what isn't.'

Anyway, she let me look for fairies.

Just to prove it, I found a fairy footprint. I
said it was, but she said it wasn't. Only I showed
her the hole the fairy came in by, and I think
that half convinced her.

Then a big man came in the barn.

'Ruth?' he said.

'Hello,' I said.

'Hello yourself,' he said, very cheerfully, holding out his hand. 'The name's Gettigan. Paul
Gettigan. And this must be wee Katya!' He made
a move at her, but Katya squirmed away behind
me, with her finger in her mouth.

'That one would be the daddy's delight!' he
said. 'Red hair and green eyes, like yourself!'

Big smile at me, and all the time I was wondering *who is this Paul Gettigan one?*

I didn't say a word.

I was sizing him up. Big man, smart jeans, white shirt, leather jacket, and yellow shoes that already had cow's muck on them from our yard. Not a country one then. No country one would be seen dead in a pair of soft shoes like that.

'You don't remember me then, Ruth?' he said.

I shook my head.

'You were no size when I last saw you!' he said. 'And look at you now. A fine strong girl!'

A solid lump of a girl, he meant, that was what went through my mind. I'm not one of the thin kind, I'm built solid like my mother. I wasn't too pleased to find I had a blush on. I get blushes whether I want them or not, especially with strangers. The blushes are a terrible bother to me.

James came in.

He stood there, looking at the man.

'This is James,' I said, politely.

'James!' said the man. 'Paul Gettigan's the name. How-do?'

'Is that your van?' James said.

'It is.'

'Can I have a ride in her?' James said, hopefully.

I gave him a look. If looks could have killed he would have been dead and buried and arguing it out with St Peter up above.

'You are very cheeky, James!' I said, quickly, because I have enough civility in me to know that begging favours is no way to be greeting anybody, and the man was a stranger to us.

'Oh, I don't mind!' the man said. 'A ride might just be arranged.'

He hadn't got far with me, so he started talking to James about engines, and before I knew it the pair of them were out in the yard in front of the house with the bonnet of the van raised, talking nineteen to the dozen. The way James tells it now, he was *finding-out*, but that wasn't the way of it at all.

My mother came out into the yard, with a slip of a girl with her. The girl was in blue jeans with a yellow top, and she had bright shiny hair that must have come out of a bottle. First of all I thought she was about nineteen, but when she got nearer I caught sight of the wrinkles round her chin, and added on another nought. Not one hundred and ninety . . . twenty-nine. Old, anyway. An old one dolled up to look like a young one, with heavy stuff on her face that would wash off in the bath.

'Ruth?' Mum said.

I came out of the barn towards her.

'This is Mrs Gettigan, Ruth,' she said.

'Paula,' the woman put in. 'You must call me Paula.'

'Oh well,' Mum said. 'Whatever you like.'

It wasn't *what* she said.

It was the way she said it.

One sudden flash of fire and brimstone!

I thought, *well, that's pinned her ladyship's ears back for her and no mistake!*

Mum was raging mad.

Only not *raging* mad.

Whatever it was, she was holding it in, but I could see her hands by her sides, and her right hand was worrying at her wedding ring, and that is no good sign in our house.

'Hello, Ruth,' the woman said. 'It is great to see you again, after all this time.'

I looked at her. I didn't know her from Adam! I didn't know either of them, Paul or Paula, and there they were letting on that I did.

'Maybe you don't remember me?' she said.

'How could she?' my mum broke in.

It hung between them for a moment.

'She was in her pram,' Paula said, easily. 'And

we can't all make an impression! I don't let on to be all that memorable!' She made a joke of it, working against the look on my mum's face.

I have never *ever* seen a look on my mum's face like I saw that day. She looked fierce to bubbling, gone wild, with her colour up and her cheeks flaring.

'I'd remember you anywhere,' Mum said, just like that. 'Oh, I'll remember you all right.'

She said it straight to the woman's face.

'Now then,' the woman said, looking straight back in Mum's eyes.

What did that mean? *Now then.* The way she said it it seemed to be a kind of reproach, or a warning, but what for? I was banjaxed. I couldn't make head nor tail of it.

My mum is big and easy-going and very soft with her words when she is not giving out at somebody, which she only does when she loses the bap.

Well, the bap was lost.

'I think we'd better have another talk, before anything happens that you might regret,' the woman, Mrs Gettigan, said.

And she took my mother . . . she *took* my mother . . . she took my mother by the arm, and kind of pulled her round.

The way Mum was looking I thought she would eat the head off Mrs Gettigan all at once, one sitting, but she didn't.

They went back in the house.

I felt Katya tugging at my hand.

'Ruth?' she said.

'Oh never bother me now, wee thing,' I said, because there I was, half-distracted, wondering what on earth was going on around me.

'Who are that man and that lady, Ruth?' Katya said, looking up at me.

'It is all right, pet,' I said. 'They are Mammy's friends.'

I didn't believe it, but it is not the kind of lie I could blame myself for. It was just like telling her that there were fairy footprints in the barn, and a door the fairies came in by.

A lie to keep her happy.

You have to tell stories to little children sometimes.

Chapter 3

Mum and Mrs Gettigan were in the front room, with the door tight shut, and James and Katya were out with the man in the yard.

There was no call for me to be hanging around, so I went upstairs to my room and sat down at my table by the window.

I wasn't worried too much . . . that came later. Then I was just puzzled by it all. These people, Paul and Paula Gettigan, turning up out of the blue, saying they were old friends come to visit us. While we had been up at the Long Woman's Stone they had been in the house with my mum, and something had passed between them that had changed her from being her usual cheerful self to a wedding ring twister with flushed cheeks.

Something was going on.

What sort of something?

I hadn't a clue. It would be grown-up stuff.

I ended up lying on my bed over from the window and looking out over the fields at the water breaking on the rocks, just hoping the Gettigans would clear off with whatever they had come for settled, and let things get back to normal.

Then James came and put his head round the door.

'Ruth?' he said.

'What is it?' I said. I had no time for James just then. He had been so busy showing off all he knew about car engines to Paul Gettigan that he hadn't stopped to think why Mum was behaving so oddly. Hadn't noticed, I expect. So much for the big detective book expertise.

'We're to move the cows out of the two low fields, Ruth,' he said.

'What for?' I said, surprised, because it was only a day since we'd moved them down there, and it made no sense to me at all.

'I don't know,' he said. 'Mum just came out and told me. So we are to do it.'

'I'll speak to Mum,' I said, and I got off the bed and clattered down the stairs.

Mum was at the door to the front room.

'D'you really want the cows moving?' I said to her.

'Do what you're told, Ruth,' she said.

'But . . .'

'I am telling you to do what you are told, and ask me no questions!'

I looked at her, letting her see my nose was out of joint. Why wouldn't I? Moving the cows *was* a daft thing to be doing.

'Okay,' I said. 'Keep your hair on.'

Then I was sorry for saying it.

I knew what it probably was. Probably she had something that wanted saying to this Paul and Paula and she didn't want us in on it. That would be the only reason I could think of for moving the cows when there was no call to move them. It would have James and me out of the house and busy for twenty minutes or so, and maybe by the time we got back whatever was going on would be over.

That's what I thought, so I didn't argue any more. I went out of the house and got my cow switch from the porch and went out over the wall, cow-whooping.

James was down the front field before me, and beyond him again, in the low field, the field above the McRoberts' bungalow, was Mr Paul Gettigan making an ass of himself.

There were only the eight bullocks in the low

field. They should have given him no bother at all, but he hadn't a clue which way to turn. I sent James over the wall after him to bail him out, and I went after the rest myself.

So whatever the big talk-in was in our front room Mr Gettigan wasn't in on it. Just Paula. Paul and Paula. Silly names. Did you ever hear the like?

Well, the Paul one got himself into the soft bit behind the bungalow, which didn't do his fancy yellow shoes one bit of good. He was after one bullock, while James was already yahooing and blathering at the others, running them up towards the gate. Then James had them through the gate and heading off up the front field, and I went up to join him by the wall.

'Do you know why we're moving the cows, James?' I asked.

James nodded towards Mr Gettigan, who had got himelf out of the mud, and was chasing after the young bullock, who must have thought he was soft in the head.

'He told the woman, and the woman told Mum,' James said.

I took that in.

'Mrs Gettigan *told* Mum to shift Murnaghan's cows?' I said, slowly.

'He told her, and she told Mum,' James said.

Curiouser and curiouser.

'What does he know about cows?' I said, not able to keep the puzzlement of it out of my voice.

'Maybe he is from Mr Murnaghan,' James said, and then he was off down the field after one of the bullocks, which had taken it into its head to cut back on us.

The man came through the yard gate, with the last bullock loitering in front of him, tail swishing with the flies.

He was a sight. His shoes and socks and his nice clean jeans were all mucky, and he didn't look one bit pleased. He must have known he'd made a fool of himself trying to copy James and run round whooping with his stick, trying to act out that he was a big countryman. You only had to look at the cut of him to know that he was a city man, born and bred, making out that he was a cowboy.

'You'd a hard time there, Mr Gettigan,' I said.

I had decided I wasn't *Paul-ing* him yet, till I had an idea what he was up to.

'I haven't your expertise,' he said, giving me a

25

big smile that was supposed to flatter the wee girl and put me at my ease. Didn't work though! I am not that easy got round.

'You're not from Mr Murnaghan?' I said, innocently. There was no reason why he should be, except that he was apparently giving Mum orders about the Murnaghans' cows, but he just could have been a dealer the Murnaghans had wished on us. You would never know with old Murnaghan. He has his fingers in a lot of strange pies. Some kind of cow-dealer dressed like a city man, who just happened to be an old friend of the family?

'Murnaghan?' said the man. 'Who is that?'

'The cow-man,' I said. 'The man that owns the cows.'

'I thought they were your cows,' he said.

'We just mind them.'

'Is that the way of it?' he said. 'I wouldn't know. I'm no cow-man.'

'I didn't think you were, from the way you were letting out after them,' I said. Maybe James had got it wrong about him telling Mum to move the cows. Why would he want to do a thing like that?

We went across the yard in front of our house

together, with him picking his way round the cow pats. James was already herding them round the side of the house, up to the back field.

'Do you not get lonely out here?' he said, suddenly, looking down at the Green Harbour below, and beyond it at the blue sea, which was all a-glitter in the sun.

'No,' I said.

'It is a grand spot,' he said. 'But a bit isolated.'

'Well, we like it,' I said.

I wasn't going to defend Dooney's rocks to him. The headland is *our* place. We've been here since James was three, a year before Katya was even thought of. It is a bit out of the way, but that has its plusses and its minuses.

'All done!' James said, presenting himself as we came over the wall. He was looping the wire gate.

'I was thinking with your father away so much . . .' the man said.

'He's in England!' James said, butting in on the conversation.

'You've no manners, James,' I told him, automatically.

'So there is just your mother here on her own,

and the three of you?' Mr Gettigan said. 'Does your father come back often?'

'He's not here just now,' I said.

'He's in London, at the building,' James said. 'He has his own gang, and his own van, and they are round all over the place.'

'The Lump?' the man said.

'That's it!' James said, before I could stop him.

James should have known better than to go admitting a thing like that. There's no call to go round the ABC of it, but for those who don't know the Lump is a way of working casual self-employed and getting round the Taxman and the Insurance man. There are times when Dad does it with his gang, and times when he is properly employed with McAlpine's and the other big ones, particularly the Irish ones. On the big jobs he is legal and above board, but not all the jobs are like that, and he says you have to take what you can get where you can get it, and not make too many difficulties.

Maybe it was that they'd come about.

If they were some kind of Government Investigators, it would explain the way Mum was acting. That was one thing, and ordering our cows around was another.

Maybe I had been right the first time. Mum had put us to moving the cows simply to get us out of the way, so she could sweet-talk the woman round.

Only . . . only they were making out they were the nice Gettigans, Paul and Paula, old friends of the family, from the time we lived down in Enniskillen.

That didn't add up!

'We're expecting Dad back anytime,' I said, suddenly.

I didn't think about it. I am not sure why I said it. Just he seemed to keep going on about us being out at Dooney on our own, and I thought it would do no harm if I put in the idea that my dad might arrive out of the blue. It was true, in a way. Any time is about the time when you can expect Dad. It isn't his fault. We need the money, and there is no way he could earn as much round here. There's lots do it. They keep a house at home in Ireland but they go off and earn their money over the water, because that is where the money is. In the construction industry, anyway. The half of Ireland is over building England. You only know my dad is back when he parks the van down at the bungalow and comes carrying his bags up our Rocky Lane, sometimes with his gang with him, and sometimes not.

I thought it was no bad thing to suggest he *might* be on his way. I didn't like what was going on with the Gettigans, whatever it was, and I was certain sure that I didn't want Mr Paul Gettigan thinking he had only a woman and a fourteen-year-old and two babies to cope with.

He went into the house, and up the stairs to the bathroom.

'James,' I said. 'Listen to me now!'

'What is it?' James said.

'It would be better if you didn't go telling that Gettigan man about our business,' I said.

'Why so?' he said.

'Because I have a feeling that he wants to know,' I said. 'That's why. We know nothing about him, but from the cut of his fancy clothes and his yellow shoes he is not that great a friend to anybody like us.'

'Mum says she knows him,' he said.

'Y-e-s,' I said, considering. 'But we don't know how Mum knows him, or what she thinks of him. He might be somebody we don't want to see at all around here.'

James didn't look very convinced.

'You get all sorts at the building,' I said, and that impressed him a bit more, because it is one of the things my dad says, and he picked up on that. James always does. He is Dad's biggest fan.

'Like . . . who could he be, that we don't want to see?' James said, still bothered a bit at it.

'Like I-don't-know-who,' was all the answer I could come up with.

Anyway, it planted the idea in James' head that Mr Paul Gettigan was something to do with the building business, and that my dad might not want him coming sniffing round our place, which was what I wanted to plant, just to be on the safe side till I got talking to Mum.

Mind you, I didn't believe it myself.

Paul Gettigan had soft hands on him. There was no way he'd ever dug a road, or taken his turn with a pick and shovel.

Still, I didn't mind James thinking that was it.

Chapter 4

The next thing to do was obvious. I had to get Mum on her own and find out what was going on.

That should have been easy, but it wasn't. Mrs Gettigan had Mum closeted with her in the front room.

I had to get *in* the room, before I could do anything. Then maybe I could get Mrs Gettigan *out*, and Mum and I could do some talking.

Brainwave!

I went into the kitchen, and made two cups of instant coffee, one for Mum and one for the Gettigan woman. Then I realized I'd got it wrong. If I walked in with just the two cups saying I'd made the coffee for them, I would have no excuse to linger on. So I made a third cup for me, and then I had another rethink, and made a *fourth* cup for Paul Gettigan. I didn't want them thinking I was uncivil, just because I've been brought up in the back of beyond.

I took his coffee out to the yard. He was busy at the back of the van, unloading something.

'What's that you're at?' I said, playing up to him.

'A surprise!' he said, giving me a big grin.

He had a big grey box thing, about the size of a TV set. He went off to our barn with it, leaving the coffee sitting on the roof of the van.

I was torn two ways. I wanted to know what he was up to, and I wanted to get in to my mum.

I picked the coffee off the roof of the van and went after him, into the barn. James was with him. They were chattering together up in the loft, with a pile of wires and stuff that I don't understand, coming out of the man's boxes. There were three of the boxes.

'I brought your coffee after you, Mr Gettigan,' I said.

'Oh, thanks a million!' he said, but he didn't come down the ladder to fetch it, so I went up.

He had the grey box open, and there was a metal panel thing with dials, and wires coming out of it. He had it set on a small folding table, like campers use, against the wall of the barn.

'What are you doing?' I asked him.

'We are very busy!' James announced, importantly. James had a lead in his hands, and he was

twisting wee bits of wire to fit in a socket. The
man must have showed him how to.

'Is that some sort of stereo?' I said, because it
looked like it.

'No!' he said.

'What is it?'

'It is a surprise,' he said. 'For your dad.'

'It's a switcher!' James said. 'A switcher for
our generator!'

'Now you've given it away!' Paul Gettigan
said, with a grin.

I didn't know that we *wanted* a switcher for
our generator. Maybe we did. We have a generator because we need one to run the place.
Often enough in the winter the power lines are
down, and when that happens we go over to
the generator, and we still have electricity.
Only it isn't a proper modern generator. It is
one Dad got off some job he worked on in
Wales, and he was a whole week getting it to
go in the back shed. Dad couldn't have afforded
to buy a proper one.

'Is that why you're here?' I said, light dawn-
ing. 'To install the switcher for our generator?'

'Oh, it's not just a social visit!' the man said,
and then he was off down the ladder, and over

34

to his van, leaving me looking at the generator switcher and the generator switcher fixer, which was James making himself important.

Well, maybe that was it.

It *could* be.

It would be like my dad to meet somebody he knew in a pub and buy us a generator switcher that we couldn't afford and then not tell my mum and then the man turns up and installs it and starts asking for his money, cash on delivery.

Maybe that was the trouble.

They might be wanting hundreds of pounds for their generator switcher, and my mum hadn't got hundreds of pounds to give them!

'This is great!' James said. 'It is a big deal. It will switch the generator on and off when we want it to in the winter, and there will be no more of the old business cranking her up.'

Well, that was true enough. I have spent more time than I like to think of on my hands and knees trying to get the old thing to go, and pouring stuff into her. No doubt that is why nobody minded when the generator did a walkie from the place my dad got it. It is clapped out, he says so himself, but then we only need it now and then.

35

So why did we need expensive-looking gear to switch a rotten old banjaxed generator on and off? The last thing I knew my mum had been trying to get him to chuck it away, because it was more bother than it was worth. Now we had a man and a woman and a van all come to install it, and big conferences in the front room about how to pay for it!

Then I remembered the rest of the coffee and Plan One, which was to get in on my mum.

I left them to their installation work and went back to the house where I got the other three coffees and knocked on the front room door, with a tray and biscuits and everything, as if butter wouldn't melt in my mouth.

'Come in!'

I went in, and put the tray on the table.

Katya was with Mrs Gettigan, and they were together on the sofa, playing some game with sweeties. Mum wasn't there! So much for Plan One.

'I brought you some coffee,' I said, handing her the cup. 'Would you take a biscuit?' And I handed her the plate with the biscuits on it.

'I want a biscuit!' Katya said, and the woman laughed and fed her one.

'Where's Mum?' I asked her.

'Upstairs, I think,' Mrs Gettigan said, and she got Katya up on her knee and bounced her, biscuit and all, beaming at us both.

She didn't act like she was just after a we-want-our-money-for-the-job-or-else conversation.

'I'll take the coffee up to her then,' I said, making for the door.

'I wouldn't do that if I were you, Ruth,' she said. 'Your mother is having a lie down in her room for a minute. I don't think she wants to be disturbed.'

'Oh, I'll not disturb her!' I said, but I made sure I said it going out the door, so there was no time to argue it.

The way she'd said *I wouldn't do that* wasn't advice, it was an instruction. It got my dander up. So I wasn't to go and see my own mother in my own house when I wanted to! I wasn't standing around to discuss a proposition like that!

Up the stairs, and I knocked on Mum's door.

'Mum?' I called.

There was a long silence, then a shuffle.

'Who is that?' she called.

Who else could it be but me? I thought, and I couldn't figure it out at all. She knew it was me, she must have. So why didn't she just open the door?

'It is me, Ruth. Sure you know it is me!' I said, and I opened the door myself with the non-coffee cup holding hand.

She was lying on the bed with her shoes off, and her old wrap around her. She had the window open, and it was chilly enough even though it was a sunny August day.

'Are you all right?' I said.

'Me!' she said. 'Fine!'

She didn't look fine.

Her face was all puffy.

'Your face is all puffy,' I said.

'I've a cold coming,' she said.

Well, I've seen a face like that before many a time and it has nothing to do with colds.

'You've been crying,' I said, flat out, just like that, because there was no point in beating about the bush, and I wanted her to *know* I knew, and not treat me like a silly baby who has to be protected from things.

'I have not indeed,' she said. 'It's just the cold in my eye, making it stream. Maybe . . . maybe you could close that window for me?'

It must have been you that opened it I thought, but

I did it just the same, and then I went over and sat on the end of the bed and put her coffee on the bedside table beside her.

'What's so bad that you can't tell me what it is?' I said. 'It is *them*, isn't it? You were all right this morning till they came, and ever since then you've been acting strange and upset. And I *want* to understand it, because maybe I can help.'

No reply.

'I can understand things,' I said. 'I'm not a baby like James!'

There was a reproach in that, because it annoys me sometimes when she won't say things that are worrying her to me, but I was too worried to be thinking of that. I only had to look at her to know it wasn't just some row about paying for expensive switch gear my dad had bought in a pub, but not paid for.

'There's . . . there's not a thing the matter, Honest Injun!' she said, sitting up on the bed.

I put my hand on her foot, and stroked it. She likes that. She wriggled, and curled her toes.

'There is really nothing the matter, Ruth,' she said. 'Nothing you can do anything about, anyway.'

'Which means there is something the matter,' I said.

Long pause . . .

'Yes, there is,' she said.

'Well, I knew there was. Who are these people and what are they doing here and why has everything gone wrong all of a sudden?'

'I don't want to talk about it!' she said. 'All right?'

She closed her eyes, and gave a big sniff, and then she started groping beneath her pillow for a hanky. I gave her mine, silently.

She blew her nose loudly, then she wiped her cheeks. They were burning again, bright red. She has a pale skin that goes with the red hair, just like me, but when she is upset the cheeks burn.

'You are making me feel I'm no use!' I said, half-accusingly.

'I'm not going to tell you about it,' she said. 'It's a grown-up thing, Ruth.'

'And I'm not grown-up?' I said, resentfully.

I waited.

There was no point in pushing her. If she was going to tell me anything she would come to it herself.

'You *are* grown-up,' she said. 'Well, almost. You are grown-up enough not to bother me with questions when I need time to think.'

'All right,' I said.

'What I want you to do just now is *nothing*. Do you understand? You are to keep a special eye on Katya and an extra special eye on James and stop them worrying, and you are to do nothing until I've had my think and I tell you what to do. Are you with me? Do you understand?'

'I don't understand, but I'll do it,' I said.

'Mind them *especially*,' she said. 'The two wee ones.'

And then she started to cry again. It was terrible.

She had me frightened.

She just isn't that kind of person. My mum sticks up for herself. She has to because so often when things go wrong my dad isn't there, and she has to sort them out for herself. Like the time there was the trouble with Uncle James Maguire about the land my father bought off him at Timaho. It was my mother got him to stop badmouthing us round all the pubs in Goatstown. She just whirled into his house and whirled round him and whirled out again. I don't know what she said to him and Margaret Ellen, his wife, but the next Sunday they were up to us in Church and making sweet as pie, and there has never been a bad word out of them about my father since. That is the way she is. A strong person, not a weepy one.

'I'll . . . I'll speak to them again,' she said.

What did that mean? I was going to ask her, but then I didn't. She was tired and confused and upset, and there was no point in making things worse for her. Whatever the trouble was it was Big Trouble, and she would tell me in her own good time.

'Well,' I said. 'Will I put the dinner on?'

'Yes,' she said. 'Good girl yourself.'

'For . . . ?'

'Six.'

'They'll be staying over then?' I said.

Pause.

Longer pause.

'They'll be staying till they want to go,' she said.

'Yes,' I said.

Mum lay back on the bed, and closed her eyes.

'Yes, well, I'll go and peel the potatoes,' I said, and I went.

Mrs Paula Gettigan must have heard me coming out of my mum's room and down the stairs. She came out of the front room and into the kitchen carrying the tray with the cups and biscuits.

'How is your mother?' she asked me.

'Fine,' I said.

'You didn't drink your coffee,' she said.

'I have the dinner to make,' I said.

She stood looking at me for a moment, and then Katya called her from the front room, and she went back into whatever game they were playing. It was some kind of hunt-round-the-sofa, I think, from the noises that drifted across the hall.

The Gettigans were great ones for playing up to children, it seemed. She'd even brought a sweetie bag for the purpose.

I'd no way of knowing it then, but playing-with-the-children was all part of it too.

Chapter 5

I was busy with the rissoles when Mum came down the stairs. She stopped in the doorway, looking at us.

'Would you come into the other room a minute, please, Mrs Gettigan?' she said to the woman. 'I think I need to have another word with you.' She had dropped the 'Paula' too, so much for them being old pals!

Mum had pulled herself together which was a relief. She was back on her feet, and sounding determined. It soothed me a bit, but not entirely, because I still didn't know what it was that could have upset her so much.

The woman moved Katya off her knee and on to the floor, and she went out into the hall and across to the front room with my mum. I heard the door closing firmly behind them.

I never let on that I thought it was anything special. I didn't want James or Katya to see how worried I was. With Mum both worried and at high doh, there was no point in having them upset. That wouldn't help anybody.

James and Paul Gettigan were getting quite pally on the sofa. James was explaining a puzzle thing from one of his detective books, about how to spot some crook. Mr Gettigan was taking him very seriously. James started showing him how the code messages in the book worked. There was a message like, 'MEET ME AT DOOM COTTAGE. THE BOSS.' and you had to decode it. You got marks for getting it right, and if you got enough marks on the problems in the book, the book told you you were a Sherlock Holmes or a Top Detective or something. There are eight of those books, and James has worked his way through the lot.

Then Mrs Gettigan came back into the kitchen. She went over and said something in Paul Gettigan's ear.

'You keep on with it, son,' Paul Gettigan said. 'I'll be back in a minute.'

Both Gettigans went across the hall to my mum, closing the door again.

They were still in there talking when I had the food ready. I had to go and knock the door to get them out.

'This is really splendid,' Paul Gettigan said, looking down at the two rissoles and the carrots and boiled potatoes I'd dumped on his plate. I had overboiled the vegetables, and it wasn't, but I didn't let it fuss me.

'Nothing beats home cooking!' Mrs Gettigan said.

Mum sat and ate. She didn't say a word. I kept trying to catch her eye, but she avoided my look.

Then an awkward thing happened.

The telephone went.

We may not have many modern things because of living out in the backwoods, but we absolutely have to have a telephone. It was the one thing Mum insisted on before we came here five years ago, because she was afraid of being miles from anywhere with two children, a three-year-old and a nine-year-old, and a baby on the way. We have it for Dad calling home, and for Mum to call him when she needs him . . . when she knows where he is, that is, which isn't exactly the same thing as when she needs him. He switches digs a lot, moving round the country where the work is, and sometimes he just sleeps in the back of the van when money is tight.

We have the telephone in the house for emergencies, but we hardly use it, so that keeps the charges down.

I thought the telephone call might be from Dad. I certainly hoped it was. My mum went to rise to answer it, putting down her knife and fork, but she was too slow.

Mrs Gettigan was out of her chair and into the hall.

'That'll be for me!' she said, quickly closing the kitchen door behind her, as if it was *her* door, and *her* telephone, and she wasn't a guest in our house.

'I didn't know you had a telephone,' Paul Gettigan said.

Nobody answered him.

I was thinking I had never seen *anyone* behave like that, when they are not in their own house.

Paul Gettigan caught the atmosphere.

He started on about what a lovely place Dooney must be to live on, with no neighbours to worry about. He kept coming back to that. I suppose it wasn't surprising in the circumstances, thinking about it now. The no-neighbours stuff was obviously very close to the forefront of his mind.

'Only the bungalow below,' James said. 'And nobody lives in the bungalow now.'

'Is that so?' Paul Gettigan said.

James started on about the McRoberts' bungalow. He told Paul Gettigan all about the people who bought it from Pearce, putting in a new floor when you only had to look at the house to know that the back wall was what needed doing. Probably the people were Belfast ones who meant to use it as a holiday house, with more money than sense. Anyway, they got their builders in and their new floor, but according to Mr Murnaghan they never showed up at the place.

The woman came back in, smiling.

'That's the call we were expecting,' she said to the man.

Click in my head.

The call we were expecting from her.

I didn't know you had a telephone from him.

Our telephone wire comes across the estuary, not over the bridge, and it runs up the back of the island beyond the Long Woman's Arm, which explains why they hadn't spotted it. It didn't explain the telephone call *she* said *they'd* been expecting coming on a telephone *he* didn't know we'd got.

Neither of them batted an eyelid, and I didn't let on that I had picked it up.

'Well, it looks as if we'll be here for a day or two, Eileen,' Mrs Gettigan said. 'That's if you manage to put us up?'

'That's no trouble,' my mum said, looking up. Then she caught me looking at her. 'No trouble at all,' she said, but she couldn't manage the smile that should have come with it.

'We'll be out of your way as soon as *possible*,' Mrs Gettigan said, coldly.

Nothing happened for the rest of the meal.

We just ate it, and then James and I did the washing-up, and then I said to James come-on-let's-go-down-to-the-harbour because I wanted to get out of the house, and off we went before anyone realized what we were at.

It was a bright clear evening, and we took our time wandering down the lane, past the side wall of McRoberts' old bungalow and then over the track and down to the old buildings by the harbour. James took off his shoes and went for a paddle on the shingle bit. I sat on the crane jetty, watching him.

It used to be a jetty for loading stone. There was mining for hardcore stuff round at the quarry, and a little pulley bogie system that brought the stone down from the quarry to the boats in the harbour. There are three or four little houses, stone-built, across the other side of the harbour, that the men lived in, and one house for the Quarry Manager, which was pulled down when the McRoberts' bungalow was put up, but that was long after the quarry stopped working, and all the men had gone away. Now the little houses are still there but their doors and windows are gone, and the slate roofs are on the slither off them. The place should look god-forsaken, but it doesn't.

It is a nice place.

The Green Harbour is really deep, and when you stand on the quay you can see right down into the water, which is clear as clear because of the rock bottom.

Just then, with the sun setting making the water shine, it looked grand.

James was paddling around in it, near the side of my dad's boat, which was pulled up high on the shingle, well above the water mark. Sometimes we go out in it, just the pair of us, on a summer night, for the herring. I'm allowed to go, because I know my way about boats. Anybody who lives out here would have to. Beyond the Armore rocks the herring is good, and one summer my dad had lobster pots, but now they are rotting in one of the old ruined houses.

James came up out from the shingle, and along the quay to me.

'You know them visitors?' he said.

'*Those* visitors,' I said. 'Not *them* visitors, James.'

'Aye, well, them,' James said.

'What about them?' I said carefully, because I didn't want to let him see how worried I was about them. Scaring James would do nobody any good.

'Mammy was shouting at them,' he said.

'Oh,' I said. 'What about?'

'I don't know, 'cause I wasn't there,' he said.

That is typical James!

'If you weren't there, how do you know she was shouting?' I said. 'If she was shouting, wouldn't we all have heard it?'

'Katya said,' he said.

'What did Katya say?' I asked.

'When we were down the field driving the cows, Katya says Mum was shouting at them,' James said.

I took that in.

'Well, that can't be right,' I said, after I had digested it. 'Mum can't have been shouting at them, because the man was with us in the fields, remember? He was down the field, and Mum was in the house with Mrs Gettigan.'

'I'm only saying what Katya said,' James said. 'I don't know.'

'I expect Katya was making it up,' I said.

But I didn't.

James settled down on the lip of the harbour wall beside me, and he started chucking pebbles down into the water, making big plops. The water was so clear you could see the stones sink all the way down.

'Why were we moving the cattle?' he asked.

I let that one ride a minute.

'Some notion of Mum's,' I said.

'It was Mr Gettigan said it to her,' James said.

'Well, I don't know,' I said, uneasily.

James did three big splashes, and then he got up and started trying his hops and steps and jumps. He saw it on the Olympics on TV, and he went round saying he was going to be a Hop-Step-Jumper but really that is only because he can't run as fast as some of the big ones in the

Primary School, and he wants to be best at something and as nobody does Hop-Step-Jumping round here it is a good one to be best at.

'Do five squares,' I said.

The square stones set on the pier are big, but I know he can do five. I thought I could put him off asking me questions I didn't know the answer to by getting him to show off his Hop-Step-Jumps.

'Easy!' he said, and he did six.

'See you try it,' he said.

I did, and I carefully mixed up my legs so I didn't make it, just to please him. Then he had to show me how. I don't think he suspected, although you never know with James. Sometimes I think he is cleverer than he lets on to be.

'That's grand gear for the generator,' he said, when we'd finished the Hop-Step-Jump competition and were back down on the shingle by Dad's boat.

'It will be if it works,' I said, sceptically. Well, I know our old generator. *Anything* that would make that work easily would be a blessing.

'Why is it set up in the barn when our generator is in the shed round the back?' he said. 'How come that thing is supposed to work our generator when it isn't connected to it?'

'Good question!' I said.

I'd been dead dumb! It had never occurred to me at all, but of course James was *right*. James and Mr Paul Gettigan had been most of the afternoon rigging the thing up all on its own in the barn at the front, charging batteries from his van and everything, but why there? Why not in the generator shed?

'I expect he'll run a line round to the generator,' I said, wondering how it could work anyway. I've never heard of a generator switch system. Where would the power come from to make it work when the power was off?

'He says it will switch the generator on and off,' James said. 'And he told me a whole lot of other bits, that I didn't understand right.'

'Uh-uh,' I said.

'I bet you wish you could Hop-Step-Jump like me!' James said.

'I can do more skippy stones than you can,' I said.

And I did. I did seventeen skips, and he only did thirteen.

'Mrs Gettigan has a foul mouth on her,' James remarked out of the blue.

Obviously his mind was still on the Gettigans.

The Hop-Step-Jumping wasn't adequate diversion.

'Oh?' I said.

I wondered what he had heard her say.

He didn't tell me.

He went all coy about it.

James is like that sometimes.

You'd think he'd never heard a bad word.

I was thinking *well, it wouldn't be the worst thing he'd hear round here sometimes*, especially when old Murnaghan and Benjy were moving the cows, but just the same I could see it had upset him. I suppose he wouldn't be used to talk like that coming from a woman. It was as well he'd never heard Mrs Cafferty down at Goatstown! Or Uncle Joe Maguire, either.

'She called Mr Gettigan an "F – B",' James said, doubtfully.

'Well, James,' I said. 'Some people talk like that. They just don't know any better.'

'Mammy doesn't talk like that,' he said.

'Uncle Joe Maguire does!' I said.

'I don't like Uncle Joe Maguire,' James said, loyally.

Nobody does much. He isn't our uncle, he's some kind of a half cousin of my dad's, but James doesn't like him because of the bad-mouthing that went on between the two families over the Timaho land and things Uncle Joe called my dad before my mum went to his house and closed his mouth for him. The Timaho land was a disaster, because Dad couldn't afford it, and it all went wrong on us.

'I don't like the Gettigans,' James said. 'I don't like them any better than I like Uncle Joe Maguire.'

I thought that that was a right one! He'd been trailing around all day with Paul Gettigan watching him set up the switch gear for our generator and reading him bits of detective books, and now all of a sudden he was turning coats.

Then I began to think.

James is cute enough, and clever.

He'd caught on to the general atmosphere. I didn't take to the Gettigans. Mum didn't like them. James had picked up the vibes, that is what it was.

'Well, I'm not too keen on them myself, James,' I said, trying to be reassuring. 'But I doubt they'll be bothering us much longer. They'll just get in their van and off on their way, and everything will be all right, and just the way it was before.'

He thought a bit.

'Only our generator will switch on and off when we want it to in winter,' he said.

'Yes, James,' I said.

I was thinking it was something I wouldn't be counting on, just the same.

Chapter 6

I wanted a closer look at our new generator switch gear, and I wanted a quiet look at it, without either of the Gettigans snooping after me.

It was easy enough. I took Katya out into the yard by-the-way to get her Horsey, rounding things up before her going-to-bed time. She goes to bed about eight, and it was a quarter to, so it was all innocent enough, and not pass-remarkable.

I had decided I was going to do everything just the way I always do everything, and never let on that I knew something was wrong. That way the Gettigans wouldn't be paying heed to me, and if there was anything I had to do, I might be able to do it.

What sort of thing was I thinking I might have to do?

It was all jumbled up in my mind then, though it became clearer later.

I don't think that *then* I had any clear notion

of what I might do, just the feeling that I had to keep my eyes and ears open and act dumb so they would take me for innocent like James and Katya, and not work out that I was half grown-up, and fourteen.

So we got Katya's yellow Horsey and we put him to bed like we do every night, in the hole in the hedge at the side of the yard, just by the gate.

Then I took her over towards the barn.

'Where are we going?' Katya said.

'For a wee look in the barn,' I said. 'But we are not telling anybody what we are doing. Just a game for you and me, all right?'

She didn't object.

Katya likes secrets.

I got her in the barn and dumped her on the straw at the back, and then I went up to the ladder to the loft, where James and Paul Gettigan had been working on our so-called switch system, which I was beginning to think was just a fairy tale made up for our benefit, the way I'd make things up for Katya.

The thing was set up against the wall, and there was a lead like an aerial over to the corner, and out through the hole in the roof.

Why would a switch mechanism for a generator need an aerial?

James was right about it being an odd place to put the thing, if it *was* a switch system. We use the barn for the cattle in winter, but we hardly use the loft at all, only for straw. It is mainly an old crumbly place that James and Katya play in. I suppose if the switch gear had to go somewhere it was a free place, but the logical free place to put it in would have been in with the generator. There would have been no problem that I could see about having the two together, and it would stop any botheration about taking lines from it across the yard and over the roof of our house and down to the shed at the back.

It made no sense at all putting it in the barn, *if* it was a switch gear for the generator.

If it was.

I thought it *wasn't* a switch gear system for our generator at all. It was something else.

So what was it?

Dials and knobs and stuff.

I know nothing at all about weird things like that, barring the computers at school, and the language lab Sister Frances has in the old Science

Room. There were no earphones or anything, but it had a sort of radio-like look to it.

Like a receiver or a transmitter.

What would be the use of that in the middle of nowhere?

You can blow things up with a thing like that, that was my first thought, and not an unnatural one. The IRA have things like that and they tune them to their bombs and some poor soul comes along the road and the next thing he knows there is a big bang in the ditch and the road is up round him and he's a dead one.

They did that to the three UDR men down in Ferrymore. One minute they were in their land-rover in a country lane, and the next there was no landrover and no lane, just a hole in the road the size of a tennis court, and bits of bodies in the hedge.

Only . . . only I didn't think it was that, some-how.

There was too much gear about the thing in our barn loft for that.

The IRA have some class of hand-held stuff they do jobs like that with. You wouldn't catch them hiding behind a hedge with a big thing like the equipment in our loft.

The Gettigans had come, moved our cows and they'd been giving Mum orders and they'd kind of moved in and taken over, and now they had this bit of equipment up in our barn, like a transmitter.

I'd heard tell of the IRA doing things like that. Taking over somebody's house and planning an ambush on some lonely road somewhere and carrying it out from the house and then making off in the car belonging to the people in the house. Only ... *only* not our sort of house. Not out the back of nowhere.

It would be a house on a road that went somewhere, a road the police or army might use. A road with two ends to it, so they could make their getaway when the job was done. Not out on a peninsula, with a one-way track that *no one* would be along on the way from somewhere to somewhere else. In all the time we've been here the army has only been out the Wrack Road once, and that was some ones that got confused because they didn't know where they were. They were English soldiers, and they only came as far as the Black Rocks and then they knew they were wrong and went back. We saw them from the house, but we weren't speaking to them.

Somebody had been switching the road signs round to confuse them, that is what that was.

So our place scarcely had the makings of a place for an ambush.

Not the IRA then.

I felt pretty certain about that, and as it turns out I was right. I suppose they just didn't *feel* like the IRA either. Not that I *know* that, for I have no way of knowing, not being in with that sort, but there are enough people around here who might *think* that way, and you kind of take it in with your mother's milk. For all they say in the papers, the IRA are *ordinary* ones, and the Gettigans weren't like that. They were *flash*, him with his yellow shoes and his leather jacket, and her with her made-up face you could leave foot-prints on if you were a fly that landed on her nose. Anyway, all I can say is I knew the Gettigans weren't the IRA. In a way it would have been easier if they had been the IRA, because that is something I'd have understood. Nothing has ever happened to us, that way, but living where we do it is the sort of thing you take on board as being something that *might* happen, even when it doesn't.

I went down the ladder.

'BOO!' Katya said, poking her head up out of the straw.

'Boo-you!' I said, not pointing out to her that if her head was in the straw her big bottom in its blue jeans was sticking out the other end, so I was hardly as surprised as I might have been.

'What'll we do now, Ruth?' she said.

I was thinking, *that's a good question!*

I hadn't a clue what to do now.

'Well, I want a word with your Mammy!' I said.

'I want one too,' she said.

'Well, you are just going to play in the yard a minute before I put you to bed,' I said.

'I am not!' she said.

'You'll do what you're told!' I snapped. Really I shouldn't have, but by this time I was a bit worked-up, and I suppose I let it out on the child. It was all difficult, because there was all this I-didn't-know-what going on around me, with Mum and the Gettigans and the thing in the loft, and at the same time I felt the need to act ordinary because of James and Katya.

'You be a good girl,' I said to her. 'I really really want to talk to Mum for a minute and then I'll come out and bring you a drink and a biscuit and you can have it up on the wall.'

'No,' she said, and she put her arm round my leg, just above the kneecaps, and clung on.

'Please, Katya?' I said.

'I don't want to,' she said.

'I don't care what you want!' I said. 'Just stay in the yard and don't bother me.'

She isn't usually all that clingy, but this time she buried her head in my knees, so I was caught with my arms on her shoulders. She almost had me over on the ground.

'Mind, pet!' I said, and I plucked her up. 'What's the matter?'

'I'm sick,' she said.

'What sort of sick?'

'In my legs,' she said. 'And Katya's tummy. And my head. And . . .'

The head went down against my leg again, and it was just a baby-mumble.

Sick all over, but not *very* sick.

'Would a story help?' I said.

'Y-e-s,' she said.

'Well, I tell you what,' I said, abandoning notions of getting to Mum till I had her quieted. 'I'll take you up and wash you and do your teeth and we'll put you to bed and then you'll get a story.'

'Story first!' she said.

'Washing first,' I said. 'Then bed, then story.'

'No!' she said.

'Oh but yes!' I said, and I had her up in my arms out of the yard and up the stairs to the bathroom, where I topped and tailed her. Then I put her to bed and then we had our story, and another one, and then I left the light on for her and got her a glass of water and told her I'd skelp her alive if she came out, and that was it.

Mum wasn't in her room.

She was downstairs in the front room with James and the two Gettigans, all watching TV in silence.

Tight silence.

I looked in, but I didn't go in on them.

I was stood in the hall, with the telephone beside me.

Suddenly my head was racing.

The TV was up loud, and I closed the door, cutting the noise out.

I was wondering if they could hear the dialling sound, and I thought that there was no way they could.

I picked up the phone.

No dialling tone.

No nothing, not even a buzz.

Dead.

It wasn't dead at dinner-time I thought, and it didn't take me much more thinking to work out how it could be dead now.

I went out into the porch, and round the back, to see if the line was cut there, but it wasn't.

The Gettigans would be too clever for that.

It is a long line.

The cut would be somewhere up over the Long Woman's Arm, beyond the Shoulder, where we couldn't see it from the house.

One of them must have been out for a walk, while James and I were down at the harbour. Out for a walk with Paul Gettigan's pliers from his tool kit in the van.

Well, they must be crooks, but they weren't so smart as they thought they were.

There's more than one way to get help, once you know you really need it.

We *needed* it.

I needed a whole clatter of big policemen to put a stop to their carry-on, whatever it was.

Chapter 7

I waited till the light started to go, just sitting in my room, wishing I could tell Mum, but I couldn't. The Gettigans were making sure of her, but they didn't think I was a danger to them. Well, they had another think coming!

The first move was a spot of fence-busting at the corner of the top field. One of the old posts there is rotten, and I juggled it about like a broken tooth till it came down, sufficiently for my purpose.

Then I had to get the old bullocks to move. I *needed* them to move, but I couldn't yell and yahoo at them the way I normally would, because the last thing I wanted was to be spotted driving them. They had to get out on to the Shoulder and spread out over the rough ground beyond the Long Woman's Stone all on their own.

There is nothing as thrawn as a bullock. If it takes into its head that you want it going one way, it'll head another. Still, I managed it. I had three of them out, and sure enough the rest drifted after.

That was my alibi taken care of.

I went back to the house, and along the bank at the back, behind the front room window.

Then I started yahoo-ing, as loud as I could, and I banged on the back window. If I disturbed their TV watching it was nothing more than they deserved, and not half the disturbance they were going to get before I was through.

Mum pulled the window down.

'The old bullocks are out the back field on to the Shoulder!' I said. 'I'm away after them.'

'Oh no!' she said.

'Oh yes!' I said.

'I'll be with you!' James' voice came from behind her, sounding excited.

'No . . .' I said, but I was too late.

I couldn't say, 'I don't want him with me!' to Mum, because it would have given the game away. The first thing gone wrong with my plan, and I had only started. Well, maybe I could use him. He would have to make enough noise for two, and that would keep him busy.

'Will you manage?' Mum said.

''Course we'll manage!' I said. Then I added,

'It is that old black devil again,' looking Mum hard in the face.

I don't think she twigged it, that is what I was thinking, as I came away from the window. That was a pity, because I wanted her to stall the Gettigans, in case they decided to come looking for me. We have no black bullock. Any other time Mum would have twigged it, but I suppose she had more on her mind, sitting in the room with the two Gettigans, wondering what move they would make next.

She didn't twig it, either. She told me so herself. Then she didn't know I'd got as far as I had with my thoughts on what the Gettigans were up to and neither did the Gettigans.

I didn't know what they were there for, but I knew they were up to no good, and that we needed help to sort them out.

If my plan worked, help would not be long coming. I'd have the half of Goatstown plus the RUC on their ears, and *then* they could explain why they'd moved in on a woman with children on her own and set up some kind of radio station in her barn, and altogether what they were doing. They had Mum frightened, and me frightened, and that was enough for me.

Now I had James to cope with into the bargain!

He came belting round the side of the house, with his cattle stick.

'They are over the corner of the back field, James!' I shouted at him, for the benefit of the ones in the house, if they could hear us.

Off we went.

'The fence is all broken,' James said, surveying the broken fence in the back field. 'The bad beasts!'

'Never trust a bullock, James,' I said.

They'd done me proud. They were well spread out, which meant we were *over* the Shoulder, and shielded by the long stretch of the Long Woman's Arm from the house. They wouldn't be able to see me get away.

I stopped. Time to sort James out. He didn't know what was going on, and I didn't want to tell him for fear he would give me away or get into a panic.

'Hold on a minute, James,' I said.

'What for?' he said, turning to face me.

'I want you to do something for me,' I said. 'Listen now, and don't argue, for it is important. You are to go after the cattle and make as much noise as you can, but you are not be too quick catching them. Understand? I have a wee message of my own to do, that I don't want those ones in the house knowing about it.'

James took it in.

'Why?' he said.

'Never you mind why,' I said, because I couldn't think of a why that would convince him, other than the truth, which was that the Gettigans were crooks and they had us held prisoners, more or less, on our own land in our own house, and I needed help to turn the tables on them. Mum couldn't get help, because they had their eyes on her, and therefore it was up to me to show them I wasn't just some kid they could count out of their calculations.

He opened his mouth to argue with me, but I cut him off.

'Just do it!' I said.

'But . . .'

'You'll have to trust me,' I said. 'I'll do my message and then I'll be back and then we'll have the cattle in and nobody will know. But don't you bring the cattle in till I am back. Understand?'

His small face had gone all peaky.

He didn't understand.

'They're *bad* people, James,' I said. 'I'm away over the bridge to the Coadys' to see we get some help. All right?'

'What sort of bad people?' he said.

'Well, look, I don't know,' I said, desperately. 'But I do know that I haven't time to stick here talking about it. Just you do what I say!'

He nodded.

He is a real good kid.

'Don't you go back till I'm back,' I said. 'And if one of them comes out to you, tell them I went over the other side, and one of the beasts has gone further than the rest. Okay?'

'Well, all right,' he said.

I left him standing there, holding his stick, looking very small.

I had to turn back and tell him not to stand so still because it would be a dead give-away.

Then I was off.

I felt guilty about it. I hadn't wanted him mixed up in it because he is too small, but what could I do? I had to leave him there, because I couldn't take him with me. He would never have managed the run quickly enough. It would have taken ages to get him down to the bridge, down the Black Rock Gully, and I needed my wits about me, and no small boy antics to put up with. I had to get off the island, and along the Goatstown road, either stopping a car or getting to Coadys' house, whichever came first, and then I had to get back again, before they worked out that I'd been away. The thing I was most afraid of was that they would cotton on to what I was doing, because then they would be alerted and they'd be in the house with Mum and Katya and James and I didn't like to think what might happen.

I was able to move quickly enough on my own, but it still wasn't easy. No one would ever choose to go over behind the Shoulder to the bridge, the way I had to go. It had been a toss-up in my mind between trying to sneak off on the bike round the road, and going the hard way, but the hard way had won because I was sure they would have spotted me if I'd tried to get the bike away from the house. This way, the farside of the hill, I had the cover of the Long Woman's Arm working for me, and the light beginning to go as well.

There was no way I could be spotted.

I had my mind made up to that.

The only bad bit was the gully down by the Black Rocks, but I got down that with the help of the heather and only a bit of damage to my arms and elbows, and then it was a straight run on the goatpath to the ridge above the road.

I came crashing down it and on to the Wrack road, and then I stopped.

The bridge was only a hundred yards away but there was a car parked there, a red Toyota, with someone in it. It had the lights off, but I could see the light of a cigarette.

It was a good thing the dusk had closed in, or the person in the car would have seen me.

The Gettigans weren't so trusting after all.

They'd had insurance, just in case any of us tried to get over to the mainland, and get help.

We were prisoners on Dooney, all of us.

I moved away from the humpy bridge.

It is a bridge across a narrow cut, and the tide was low. I wondered for a moment if I could get down on the shore and work my way out along the supports of the first three or four arches. Then it would be into the water . . . and I know the Cold Water well enough to cancel that idea out. The Cold Water lives up to its name, and the channel would be twenty or thirty metres across, even at low tide, and three to four metres deep of churning swirly water, the right place for a suicide, which would do nobody any good.

That's the narrow point. That is why the bridge is there.

There is no other crossing.

No crossing ... but away along the beach, where the river meets the sea and widens out ... I could try swimming it, with maybe a chance that I would make it.

No dice!

It is tricky old water that, when the river is running out and the tide is running in, full of currents and counterflows.

I would be doing no good for anyone, dead and drowned.

No way that way.

So what other way could there be?

If this had been a story in one of James' adventure books I'd have been able to flash a secret message to the mainland and the police would have come running, but I had nothing to flash with and more important still, our mainland isn't that sort of mainland. I would have looked a fool flashing S-O-S on the torch I hadn't got at the few gulls on the cliff above the Cold Water, gulls not being too clever at reading messages, or delivering them to the police.

I should have come up with something, but I didn't.

I went back to James, thinking hard. They still didn't know I was wise to them. Maybe I could find some other way to get help. I *had* to go back because of James anyway, so really I had no choice in the matter.

He wasn't acting the part I'd told him to. He was crouched by the side of the Long Woman's Stone, looking miserable.

'James! James! Are you all right, James?' I said.

'Where were you?' he said. He was looking very frightened, poor little thing. I shouldn't have told him about the 'bad people'.

'I'm sorry, James,' I said. 'I'm really sorry.'

I couldn't take him straight back to the house, because we still had to fetch the cows. He was cold and shivering by the time we had finished. I'd been longer gone that I meant to be, but it was no easy work getting down to the bridge in the first place, and then I'd wasted time trying to figure things out.

My mum was up the field with a torch looking for us, when we came back over the shoulder, driving the last of the bullocks.

'Where were you?' she said, obviously alarmed.

'I tried going for help,' I said. 'They have a man on the bridge. We can't get off the headland.'

'I know that,' she said.

'Mum!' James said, and she scooped him up in her arms.

'The wee lamb is frozen,' she said.

'Who are the Gettigans, Mum?' I said. 'What are they going to do?'

She gave me a not-in-front-of-the-child look, and she started hurrying me back to the house.

"*Mum . . .?*" I said.

'I'm thinking *it!*' she said. 'Just . . . just act normal and don't do *anything*. Don't you dare do a stupid thing like that again.'

'But . . .'

'They have their eye on you already,' she said. 'That's bad enough. But the two little ones . . .'

Then she had to stop.

Paul Gettigan had come round the back of the house, flashing a torch. He picked us out in its beam.

'They're all right!' Mum said, going past him.

I was following her, but he put an arm on my shoulder and squeezed hard, stopping me.

'You are a very foolish girl,' he said.

He was grinning all over his stupid face.

'The cows . . .' I said. 'The old bullocks got out of the field and . . .'

My voice faded away.

My mother had gone round the side gable of the house, hurrying to get James into the warmth. We were on our own in the field.

He put his hand in his coat pocket, and pulled something out.

'See this?' he said.

It was a gun.

I just stared at it.

'It goes off if you pull the trigger,' he said. 'Do you understand?'

'Yes.'

'Your mother has two small children in there,' he said. 'You wouldn't want anything happening to them, would you?'

'No.'

'Well then, be a good girl and behave yourself,' he said.

'Yes,' I said.

'Good,' he said.

Long pause.

'Paula has the kettle on for a cup of tea,' he said. 'When we heard you'd been all the way to the bridge and back, we thought you might be needing one.'

I didn't say anything to that.

They knew I'd been to the bridge, so all my creeping about hadn't been that clever. Either the man at the bridge had spotted me, or there were more of them or . . . or . . . if the switch mechanism was some kind of radio gear it would account for them knowing where I'd been. The man at the bridge could have radioed them back that he'd seen me . . . or the other men, if there were other men.

We went into the house.

Paula Gettigan had the tea tray all laid, with a cloth and all, and four cups, and biscuits out of my mother's tin. She was making the house her own.

'Well?' she said to the man.

'Ruth understands now,' he said.

It just boiled up in me, suddenly. I was cold and tired and very frightened, and close to tears.

'My . . . my dad will fix you!' I said. I suppose it was a silly thing to say, but I was all het up.

'Your father isn't here,' Paula Gettigan said. 'One lump or two?'

My mum came into the room.

She took the situation in at a glance.

'If you touch that child, you'll answer for it!' she said, and she came over and grabbed me, and pulled me down on the sofa beside her, hugging me. 'Are you all right, Ruth?'

'She's all right, Mrs Maguire,' Mrs Gettigan said. 'You are all going to be all right, if you just behave yourselves and do exactly what you are told.'

'We won't disturb you,' Mum said bitterly, and she hugged me again.

'And that goes for Ruth, as well?' Paula Gettigan said.

'I . . .'

'Ruth's a very sensible girl,' Mum said.

Mum was *shaking* as she hugged me. Absolutely shaking! I suppose it was pent-up anger and the frustration of it. There was nothing she could do.

'Well, a *sensible* girl wouldn't do anything that would harm her little brother and sister,' Paula Gettigan said. 'Am I right, Ruth?'

James and Katya were hostages for our good behaviour. Whatever the Gettigans and the others with them were up to, we just had to let them get on with it. That was the message she gave us, sitting in *our* front room, dunking one of *our* biscuits in *our* tea cup and drinking *our* tea.

They must have threatened Mum with guns at the beginning, the same way they were threatening me. It explained the way she had been acting ever since. She'd done nothing about it, because she couldn't think of anything to do.

What would I have done, in her place?

It is the kind of thing that *doesn't* happen ... at least, that's what I would have thought, until I found myself in the middle of it. A man and a woman drive up to your house and take it over by making threats against a couple of children. *Three* children really. It was my mum they'd started off threatening, not me. Mum had the three of us to consider, and she'd done ... nothing. Because there was nothing she could do. How do you cope with a situation like that if you are caught as my mum was?

I suppose Mum was too worried about the consequences to try using the telephone, before they cut the wire, or too upset even to think of it.

'I'm sure Mrs Maguire and Ruth understand the position now, Paul,' Mrs Gettigan said.

'Perhaps we should leave them together for a while? They have a lot to talk about.'

'Yes,' he said.

They went out of the room together, carrying their cups and saucers. Then he nipped back in, smiled, and took another biscuit.

'Very tasty!' he said, munching it, and out he went.

'There is absolutely nothing we can do, Ruth,' Mum said, answering the question I hadn't asked. 'Oh, pet, I'm so sorry! But we have James and Katya to think of. Keeping them safe comes before everything else.'

Chapter 9

A beautiful, quiet morning at Dooney, with the waves lapping round the rocks and the cows slumbering in the field behind the house, with nothing to worry about but the odd fly-swat with their tails.

Everything was right with the world.

Except that Mum and James and Katya and I sat down to breakfast with our two jailers, who were busily pretending to be ordinary people that we knew and loved.

James had been down the harbour to check his crab line, but he came back all round-eyed, with a story about how there was a hole in our boat, like somebody had hit it with a hatchet.

'It wasn't there yesterday!' he kept saying. 'Me and Ruth would have seen it!'

Yesterday was before I had made any attempt to get off the island, that was what I was thinking. There might still have been a chance to use the boat, if I hadn't let the Gettigans know that

I suspected them. Well, that chance was gone.

While we were eating, the post van came and went, depositing our letters in the tin box at the foot of the lane.

That was another chance missed.

We have a tin box on the post down at the foot of the lane, for the postman to put our letters in, because there is no way you could expect his van to drive up the lane given the state it is in. If I had *really* thought things out I could have put a note in the box for him.

GET THE POLICE.
THERE ARE A MAN AND A WOMAN
AT OUR HOUSE WITH A GUN.
THEY ARE THREATENING US.

Something like that.

Only I hadn't done it.

I had forgotten all about it. The post van, I mean. It comes every day. It is the only thing that does come beyond my dad on his visits or an odd hiker, or Mr Murnaghan and Benjy on a Friday to see after their cows. I suppose the post van is so much a part of the scenery that you do forget about it.

I suppose they would have had the postman watched, anyway.

James kept babbling about the boat, until I had to tell him not to speak about it because Katya was upset. She knows the boat is my dad's, and she doesn't like things happening to his stuff. He didn't shut up, so in the end I took Katya out of the house, to escape from him ... and *them*.

I couldn't stand the Gettigans sitting there at our table, eating our toast and drinking our tea.

'Where are we going, Ruth?' Katya said, blinking in the sunlight.

'I don't know,' I said, hopelessly. 'Somewhere away from this old house. Down the field!' All I had in my head was to get away somewhere where I could sit with my backside on a rock and try to figure things out – as if I hadn't been doing that half the night already, first with my mum in the front room, and later in my own room with just myself.

'I'm not allowed down the field,' Katya said, hanging back.

It was news to me. The field lies in front of our house, and Katya spends hours there playing about round the cow pats and the thistles. We can see her there from the yard, without having to be on her tail all the time.

'Who said?' I asked.

'Mum said,' Katya replied.

'Why?'

'There's men down the field,' she said.

By this time I had her up on the wall, preparing to lift her off it down into the long grass.

'There's no men in the field, Katya,' I said, scornfully. 'Sure look see, you can see there isn't.'

Sure enough there wasn't. Just the same old front field above the low field, knee-high in grass where the cows hadn't got at it, and trimmed down where they had, with the Dooney rocks sticking up here and there, and the slate roof of the bungalow beyond winking at us in the sun, only short a slate on two after six empty winters.

'There is,' objected Katya, hanging back. 'Mum said.'

Mum said.

Being translated, that meant: *the Gettigans said.* The Gettigans said there were men in the field. But there were no men in the field.

Click!

It wasn't the men-who-weren't-in-the-field the

Gettigans were worried about. It wasn't anything to do with *that* field, or the field below it. It was the bungalow.

They didn't want us near the bungalow.

'Did you *see* any men in the field, Katya?' I said. I thought there might be men *at* the bungalow, but if there were they'd been keeping well out of the way. I certainly hadn't seen any sign of movement, but then I hadn't been watching for it.

Katya shook her head.

'Well,' I said. 'Come on and we'll have a look, because I don't think there are any men in this field, or the one below it either. I don't think there are any men!'

Katya still looked worried.

'Mum won't mind,' I said, and I lifted her down into the grass, and hopped down after her bringing half the old crumbly wall with me, because I wasn't looking what I was doing.

I was taking a good squint at the bungalow instead.

Katya was happy enough. She ran off in front, with the grass scraping her kneecaps, all flying red hair, with the new tartan frock Mum had put on her catching the seeds off the tops of the dandelions.

We strolled down the field. I was busy trying to look relaxed and casual. Running Katya through the fields is something I do everyday, anyway, so why shouldn't I be doing it?

Men in the field.

Men in the bungalow.

The two Gettigans at the house, minding us, the one guarding the bridge ... three of them, doing nothing. It was the men in the bungalow who would be *doing* whatever needed doing, the business they had come for. The rest were just lookouts, or guards, set to mind us, and make sure that no one interrupted anything.

If there were men in the bungalow, how had they got there without us seeing them?

The answer to that was easy enough. James and I had been down to the harbour the night before, past the bungalow, and no one had objected. So the men in the bungalow ... if there *were* any men ... must have come in over the humpy bridge after dark fell, sometime during the night. That produced the thought that if they were there, James' trip down to the crab line must have put a scare in them. Presumably it was *after* that that the order about not going down the field had been put out, to stop it happening again.

So all my ideas last night about there just being the two of them, the Gettigans, were eye wash. The whole thing was on a bigger scale than that. What with two guards on us at the house and at least one man on the bridge and a communication system set up in the barn and telephone wires cut and everything, it had to be a big number!

We didn't get into the low field, the one just above the bungalow.

There was a shout from behind us, and Paul Gettigan appeared on the wall in front of our house, waving his arms.

I thought I could play that one back at him. I waved back, and kept on going, all innocent, as if butter wouldn't melt in my mouth. I wasn't supposed to know there was anything *not* to see at the bungalow, so why shouldn't I walk that way?

He wasn't having any of that.

He came off the wall with a leap, and headed down the field after us, giving his yellow shoes another dose of cow pat dubbin.

'What's the matter?' I said, when he came up to us.

'You were told to stay near the house!' he said.

'I wasn't,' I said.

Well, it was true. Mum had obviously been warned off, but the message hadn't got through to me except in Katya's telling of it, and I felt that that could be discounted. I wasn't worried about lying to him, anyway.

'Get back up to the house!' he ordered, roughly.

'Why?' I said.

There was a pause.

He put his hand on Katya's shoulder, and squeezed it. Then he looked at me. 'I thought you were going to be sensible?' he said.

We went back up the field, heading for the wall, a doleful little procession with Katya in front and me in the middle, and Paul Gettigan bringing up the rear, the way we do when we are herding the beasts.

I thought I could test him a bit further.

'You have Katya scared with your men in the field,' I said.

He shrugged. He was a bit out of breath, but now he had headed us off from the bungalow he wasn't too worried.

'There are no men in the field,' I said.

'Don't push me,' he said.

'Oh well, there now,' I said, and then I thought I would try my luck a bit further. 'They are digging out whatever they dug in,' I said, letting it out flatly, as though I had known all about it from the beginning, and hadn't just thought of it. 'We often wondered why there was a new floor put in an old bungalow that had no need of it, and now we know!'

His face just *went*!

I'd scored a hit!

They had buried something in the bungalow, and now they'd come mob-handed to dig it out. The only problem was that in the six years between the time they buried the stuff and the time they came to dig it out, we had moved in, smack bang above the bungalow where we couldn't help but notice any activity that went on.

'You would be better off not knowing anything, young lady!' he said abruptly.

Then he heaved Katya up on to the wall, and clambered up after her, leaving me below him in the field to think it over.

'Not seeing anything either!' he added, over his shoulder. Then he turned round and looked down at me. 'Can you not get that into your head? Nobody *wants* to do you any harm, but the more you see and the more you know, the more danger you are to us. That makes it all the more likely that something unpleasant might happen, before all this is over.'

Katya was taking all this in. By the time I hopped down into the yard off the wall, she was standing with her thumb stuck in her mouth, and her eyes gone round-looking. I had to hold myself in check, because I didn't want her to be frightened.

'I'll stay away from the bungalow, if that is what you want,' I said.

'You'll keep the little boy away from it too,' he said. 'He was a damn sight too close to it for his own good this morning.'

'Yes.'

'What happened to your father's boat could have happened to *him*,' he said.

And then he headed off for the barn.

'The man was cross again!' Katya said, reaching out for my hand.

'Yes,' I said. 'Yes, he was.'

'I don't like the man,' she said.

'He's a nice man, really,' I said, lying in my teeth, but trying to save myself from a Katya situation.

'I don't like the man,' Katya persisted. 'He was cross with Mum and he was cross with you. I want him to go away!'

'Well, he will,' I said.

Lying again.

What was I supposed to do? Tell her the man wasn't a nice man at all but he had a gun in his pocket and if things went wrong he would maybe kill or hurt her? That wouldn't have helped.

'Don't you worry, pet,' I said. 'We'll get out of this all right, you wait and see.'

'Out of what?' she said.

Me and my big feet! I'd done it again.

'I'll look after you,' I said, weaving to avoid that one, because there was no answer to it.

It didn't go down very well.

'Mum's here,' I said, verging on desperation. 'She wouldn't let anything happen to you, would she?'

Katya thought about it. Then, 'I want Horsey!'

Relief!

I got her Horsey out of his hedge bed, where we'd packed him away the night before. Poor old Horsey has had a hard life. He started off bright yellow with a red saddle and four small blue wheels, proud as punch beneath the Christmas tree, brought by Santa Claus care of Dunne's stores in Enniskillen, where I helped to pick him for her. The wheel axles had notches in them, so that the wheels could retract, and then he was a rocking-horse. Then the axle got bent and he wouldn't rock, and by the same token he couldn't wheel about properly. Dad tried to re-bend the axle, but it wouldn't work. We got him fixed in a rock-only mode and now he rocks, but he is a bit wonky, and the paint is off his saddle and he is like a drunken plastic horse, always likely to tip Katya on her small neck. Bust-up and broken or not, I was glad she had him to cling to. James is a bit the same, when he isn't being a big man. You see him standing there with the vest pulled out of his pants, twisting at it. That is, when he hasn't got his thumb in his mouth.

I was thinking that, and thinking about what Paul Gettigan had said about the boat, and maybe the same thing happening to James.

Somebody had taken a hatchet to the boat.

And I'd been almost *teasing* him, being a big detective like the ones in James' mystery books, trying to worm things out of him.

Well, I had that lesson learnt, the hard way, thinking about guns and hatchets, and the two children. My sister, and my brother . . . and I'd put them at risk with my silly detective games.

I had been childish to go on thinking I could outwit Paul Gettigan and his lady friend where it was obvious that I couldn't. Mum couldn't, and she is a sight bigger and smarter than I am.

Mum was right.

Keep the kids safe was all that we could do. I had to do just that, and back her up every way I could.

It wasn't an exciting decision, the kind of thing that one of the children in James' books would have come to, but it was a realistic one . . . a grown-up one.

I had to be satisfied with that.

It was the best I could manage.

Chapter 9

I have to hand it to my mum. She was really sensible.

What do you do when you have two people at your house with guns, ready to shoot your children?

You clean out the henhouses, that's what you do!

Some people who don't live like we do might not know what that really means.

Well, I'll tell you.

What comes out of the rear ends of hens isn't ordinary. It pongs like nobody's business. And it pongs worse when it has been undisturbed for a while, and then you take a shovel and a wheelbarrow and you go into the henhouses, one after another, and you ladle it all up, and then you dump it.

There is nothing worse than cleaning out a good henhouse full of what comes out of the back end of hens, and I don't mean the eggs!

'Oh no, Mum!' I said, when she said it.

'Oh yes, Ruth!' she said. 'Put on your oldest stuff and get the shovel, and off we go.'

So we did.

Mum and James and me.

Not Katya.

Mrs Gettigan was reading to Katya, out on the front step, a relaxed kindly auntie with her sweetie bag. It hadn't escaped anybody's notice that our city lady with her smart clothes and her thick make-up was keeping very close to the child, whenever she could. It was *let's play this, dear* and *come on and we'll play that while your mummy is busy*, skin-crawling stuff like that.

I'll hand it to Katya, she was reluctant. For all the woman was making up to her, the child didn't like her. Still, what with stories, and the bag of sweeties she kept waving under the wee child's nose, Katya stayed with her.

'You know what *that's* about?' I said to Mum.

I shouldn't have said it really, it only made things worse. Mum knew all right.

If anything happened, Paula don't-I-love-little-children Gettigan was going to have her insurance policy right under her nose. It was clever, calculated and unpleasant, because we knew she had a gun as well, she'd made that plain to Mum. So long as she had Katya with her, we were completely stymied.

The henhouses were no better and no worse than they always are, which means they were bad. James did his usual, and sat down in the muck, so Mum had to send him off. I think she'd been banking on that anyway, for as soon as he was gone, she beckoned me into the big house by the wire, which was the one they'd been working at. I'd been at the old one, down by the drain.

I went in after her.

We upturned two crates on the floor, and sat on them.

'They'll not come here,' Mum said.

'Not with this pong!' I said.

'That was the idea,' she said. 'I wanted you on your own.'

'What for?'

'Something might be going to happen,' she said.

'Oh!' I said.

'I had an idea, and I just went and did it,' she said. 'They shook me when they got onto you last night. I thought *I've got to do something*. So I did. That is why I was so quick sending

James down the lane this morning to check his crab lines. He posted something for me.'

Then I got it.

The post box! She'd thought of the post box the same way I had, only she had done something about it.

'They wouldn't think of the postman doing anything but *deliver* letters,' she said. 'They're city ones, and that is the way things go in the city.'

She was right of course.

Mr Purdy is our postman. There is no point in making us go four miles into Goatstown to post a letter. If we have one we just leave it in the tin box on the post at the end of the lane, and if Mr Purdy sees one with a stamp and all he takes it. I don't think he is *supposed* to take it, but that is the way a city postman would think of things. Mr Purdy has all sorts in his van sometimes, some of it official business and some of it not. If anybody is ill they are as like to ring Mrs Hannigan and she will have a box of groceries or a prescription made up and it will go out in Mr Purdy's post van, as if it was a letter with a stamp on it. Mr Purdy doesn't get anything out of it. He is just good-natured.

'I don't think they counted on Mr Purdy,' she said. She was awful brave to risk it, but I suppose what had happened to me the night before must have stirred her up.

'It is all right if Mr Purdy thought to look in the box,' I said.

'Well, the van was there, so he must have left something,' she said. 'So if he put something in, he'll have taken my note out, and the word should be down to Sergeant Gehan by now.'

'Right!' I said.

'If it goes right, we might get out of this in one piece,' she said.

I thought a bit.

'Would they raid the house, or what?' I said, anxiously.

'I don't know what,' Mum said. 'I'm no policeman.'

'James,' I said. 'James and Katya . . .'

'Well, they ought to know about James and Katya,' she said. 'What I'm counting on is that they *won't* raid the house, but just pick these people up when they go to leave here.'

'Yes, but what if they do raid the house?'

If that happened, it would mean James and Katya going for a ride in the van, with the

Gettigans holding guns to their heads, and the policemen having to let them go.

Mum shrugged, helplessly. She must have been feeling very desperate to risk it.

'They wouldn't shoot James and Katya,' I said. 'It is only unshot that the children are any use to them.'

Maybe it would have been better left unsaid. Mum had been very brave, and I suppose she must have worked it all out, but I wasn't sure she had done the right thing.

'What if we got hold of James and Katya, and locked ourselves all in the same room?' I said.

'There isn't a door in the house that that man couldn't put his boot through, if he had a mind to,' Mum said. 'Anyway, there is only the one lock that works, and that is on the front door.'

'If we could get both the Gettigans out of the house at the same time . . .'

'They'd break in through the windows,' Mum said.

'Well, they won't harm James and Katya because the children are their insurance,' I said lamely, because I'd said it before and it hadn't made a good impression, and there was no reason why it should now.

'I wanted you to know, anyway,' Mum said. 'In case anything was to start happening, you know?'

Then we went back to our shovelling.

James came out again and joined in.

Two minutes, and he was hen dirt all over!

Mum gave up, and we trailed back to the house.

'My, what a mess!' nice, kind, pretty Mrs Gettigan said, and she made Mum a cup of tea.

It was like that, just *unreal*.

I couldn't stand it.

I didn't stay for the tea.

I went up after James was cleaned off and I got the muck off me and changed my clothes and then I went to lie on my bed, to see if I could sort things out in my head.

Problem: If I was the police and I got a note like that, what would I do?

What *do* they do, when there is a siege, and hostages and things like that? Usually it is an Embassy somewhere and there are TV cameras and SAS men and I don't know what and you see a puff of smoke coming out a window and blat-blat-blat with tommy guns and a whole lot get killed and the Prime Minister gets on TV talking about Democracy and the Rule of the

Gun, and how well Our Boys in the Special Air Service have done.

That is when you have the like of the SAS and the Prime Minister and the TV cameras round the corner.

All we had was Sergeant Gehan and his pot belly.

Well, Sergeant Gehan has a telephone. He could get some policemen or the British Army or whatever, and he maybe would. Then what?

The man at the bridge would spot them coming, that's what.

He would be on the radio thing to the Gettigans, and they would line us up in the yard with guns at our heads.

No good.

Well, maybe they could come onto the headland some other way. I might not be able to get *off* the island over the Cold Water, but an army or a police force must have some way of getting onto a place like our headland, without being spotted.

Only . . . how?

I gave up.

I just sat at my window, looking out at the sea for a bit, and then I went downstairs.

Nice lady, lady with a gun on her, sitting with Katya, watching TV.

Nice man, kicking James' old football about with him in the yard.

And . . .

. . . nothing happened.

I made a move, just to test them, about it being the day I take the eggs to Mrs Hannigan, but they weren't having any. They weren't letting me off Dooney to go telling tales.

I went and moped on the wall.

What was the big radio thing in the barn *for*?

It couldn't be just so they could keep in touch with each other, because there are small sets you tuck up your jumper that would do that. It had to be for something else.

Like . . . like a longer distance than the wee sets could do.

Like the sets people use at sea.

Like you might use if you wanted to keep in touch with a *boat*.

Like you might be doing if you had a boat that was to come in and lift something from a deserted harbour with a good depth on her that nobody used, since the old quarry was closed down.

Sense!

But it didn't seem to help me.

I was past caring about what it was they had buried down in the floor of the old bungalow the year before we ever came to the headland. That really didn't seem to matter at all. In one of James' adventures that would have been the important thing, but then James' books didn't have real people in them. Just Uncle Bill and boys with talking parrots to create a diversion, and clues that were hidden in old parchments, and things like that.

Not the Gettigans.

Not people with guns.

Not people like us. We could get ourselves killed for nothing at all, because we'd happened to come to live in the wrong place, out on the headland with only the rocks of Dooney and a few cows and hens to keep us company.

Then Paul Gettigan came out of the barn.

'Paula?' he yelled.

The woman came out into the yard.

They had a hurried conversation.

'Mrs Maguire?' Mrs Gettigan called.

Mum came out of the house.

'We have a slight problem on our hands, Mrs Maguire,' Mrs Gettigan said.

I thought *good*. Well, I hoped it was good anyhow. Anything that set a problem for them might be an opportunity for us. What if we could get hold of Katya and James and make a run for it? We could get over the Shoulder and maybe go to ground near the castle ruins, or in one of the caves round the back, and if they couldn't find us while they were coping with their slight problem then they couldn't shoot us, or use James and Katya as hostages, could they?

'A herd of cows have just come over the bridge, and apparently they are coming this way!' Mrs Gettigan said, watching my mum's face carefully for a reaction.

She didn't get one.

Cows!

My head did another spin.

The RUC or the British Army SAS dressed as cows? It was too soon anyway, but . . .

Hiding in the middle of the cows maybe, like in a John Wayne film, with cow skins over their heads and six shooters ready to bang off?

'Oh,' Mum said. 'That'll be Mr Murnaghan.'

End of daft idea.

Old Murnaghan and Benjy, a day early in the week they were to pay the cow money. If it hadn't been such a let-down after my big adventure thoughts I would have laughed. The one person who wasn't going to rescue us with blazing six guns was Mr Murnaghan.

'Will he bring them here?'

'Well,' Mum said. 'They are his cows in the field behind the house, that we do the minding of. He has every right to bring them here, for that is the arrangement.'

Mum looked worried.

Well she might.

Expecting the SAS or something, and all we got was Murnaghan's cows!

Just another complication.

Old Murnaghan has a dodgy heart. The last thing we needed was Paul Gettigan pulling a gun on him and Mr Murnaghan having a heart attack on the doorstep, and not even a telephone to get an ambulance.

The most likely thing was that he wouldn't have a heart attack. They would simply add him to the hostages, keeping him prisoner like the rest of us.

'There is a young lad with the cows, and an old one in a beat-up car with him,' Paul Gettigan said. 'Would that be your Mr Murnaghan?'

Mum nodded.

'The young one will be Benjy,' I said.

Benjy to the rescue!

Somebody dropped Benjy on his head at birth, or something. He is big, but his head isn't all there. He wouldn't be a plus in a crisis, just another one to look after. I wouldn't have swopped him for James, if I had been looking for a helpmate.

We weren't going to be rescued after all. All that was going to happen would be that Benjy or the old man would get hurt.

Mum had reached the same conclusion.

'Mr Murnaghan has a bad heart,' she said. 'You wouldn't want him on your consciences, would you?'

In the circumstances it seemed to me a pretty soft-headed thing to say. The Gettigans weren't the sort to bother too much about consciences, judging by the way they'd set about things so far.

'Nothing need happen to the old man or his son, Mrs Maguire,' Paul Gettigan said. 'That is rather up to you, isn't it? If you and young Ruth keep your traps shut, he can come and he can go.'

He looked at the woman.

She nodded assent.

'Everything here is *normal*,' he said. 'Okay?'

'Yes,' Mum said.

'Don't encourage your cow-man friend to hang about,' Mrs Gettigan said. 'You have my meaning, Mrs Maguire? No tea and sympathy and asking after the relations, and trying to pass little messages in to the police.'

'Yes,' Mum said.

'And yourself, young lady?' Mrs Gettigan said, turning to me. 'Are you sure you understand?'

'Yes,' I said.

'Good,' Mrs Gettigan said. 'That's all sunshine then, isn't it?' She hooked Katya up in her arm. 'We'll just go and play in the front room, Katya and I, till Mr Murnaghan has gone.'

Katya looked a bit dubious about it.

'And the boy!' Paul Gettigan said.

'Me?' said James. He'd been sitting over on the wall, quiet as quiet. He is no fool. He says now that he knew what was happening. I don't believe that, but I do believe that he knew there was a whole lot wrong. They both did, Katya as well. They couldn't help but know it. They'd only to look at Mum and me.

'You do as you're told, James,' Mum said, miserably.

James and Katya and the woman went back into the house together.

'You both understand what will happen if there is any slip-up, don't you?' Paul Gettigan said.

I could have killed him. I could have killed both of them. If there had been a way of doing it I think I would have.

The cows came round the side of the Black Rocks, way below us on the Wrack Road.

'How do we explain you to Mr Murnaghan?' Mum asked him.

'Visitors,' Paul Gettigan said.

'Some visitors!' I said.

'If we judge it necessary, we can take the old man and his son as well,' Paul Gettigan said, ignoring me. 'But we don't want to. It wouldn't help us. He would only be a complicating factor, and we have enough trouble as it is with our friends on the boat.'

Click.

One more bit I'd got right, anyway. They were expecting a boat into our harbour, and it hadn't turned up on time. That was what his to-ing and fro-ing to the radio had been about.

'Ruth won't do anything and I won't do anything, so long as you don't hurt anybody. We
don't care what's going on, so long as we get out
of this with no one hurt,' Mum said, for both of us.

'Good.'

We waited, watching old Murnaghan's cows
plod-plodding along the Wrack Road toward the
bungalow. They had to pass the front of the
bungalow, before turning up the lane.

'It'll be a nasty shock for your friends at their
digging down there!' I said.

Paul Gettigan grunted, dismissively.

It was the same bright sunlit day it had
been earlier, and the whole thing was like somebody's bad watercolour painting of Irish Country
life, with the cows on the deserted road and the
big lad beating after them with his stick, and the
sea beyond, all flat and glistening, and the grey
of the Dooney rocks cutting up out of the fields.
Old Murnaghan would have had a fit if he'd
known he wasn't in somebody's watercolour, but
having guns pointed at him instead. I suppose
they must have been watching him from the
bungalow, though they would have been sure to
be careful about it. The place looked empty, like
it always was.

'Your two young children are in the front room, Mrs Maguire!' Paul Gettigan said. 'Don't forget now.'

'She hears what you are saying,' I said, answering for Mum.

'Be sure you both heed it!' he said.

Benjy started the cows up our lane, swatting at them with his old swishy stick. Mr Murnaghan came humping and bumping in the van behind him, doing disasters to his springs. He always comes in the van. I doubt if he can walk any distance these days, beyond from his bed to Meehan's bar, which is three doors down from his house in Goatstown.

'Look,' I said. 'I'll have to go and do the gate for them, and on down to meet them. It is what I always do.'

'Have to?' asked Paul Gettigan.

'It *is* what she always does,' Mum said. 'You want things to look *normal*, don't you?'

It was true enough. We don't get many visitors out at Dooney, and it is the same routine every time old Murnaghan comes.

'Keep it relaxed,' Paul Gettigan said, giving way, but looking none too happy about it just the same.

'You mind what the man says, Ruth!' Mum said.

It was a firm order, but there was no need to give it.

There was no way I could call on Benjy and Mr Murnaghan to do anything to help us, with James and Katya holed up in the front room with a woman and a gun.

Fine chance there would have been anyway, trying to get Benjy or old Murnaghan to understand anything by slipping them notes or talking to them out of the back of my hand. They are good country people, as cow-men go, but they are none too quick on the uptake when it comes to city things, like sieges and hostages and the kind of mess we were in.

I opened the gate, heaving it over the bump in our yard so that Benjy could drive the cattle through and up to the back field. I was thinking I would have to explain to him why the cattle weren't in the fields in front of the house, where we were supposed to have them. That had been the arrangement, but the Gettigans had changed it to keep us away from the back of the bungalow.

I'd need a good excuse.

What sort of excuse?

I was still working on variations of that as the cattle came lumbering up the lane, penned in by the deep banks of the stone ditch on either side, with big Benjy hopping and dancing and cursing at them, swiping with his stick at their fat backsides.

Whoever he was, he did it real country style.

He must have been a born actor.

The *real* Benjy Murnaghan couldn't have done it any better.

Chapter 10

'Hiya Benjy!' I sang out.

'Good girl yourself, Ruthie!' he whooped, and he scooped me up in his big arms, all dark and hairy. He was a big fellow in a woolly green cardigan and baggy pants, with huge clod-hoppy boots on him. He was like enough to Benjy at a distance.

'The woman has the two children in the front room of our house and she has her gun with her,' I said. 'You are not to do anything at all.'

'Right you are then, Ruthie!' he said, and he whirled me round and dumped me down and then he was off swaggering up the lane, yelling and screaming that the cows were bad beasts and he'd see them in hell if they didn't get on their way to the field.

I waited for the one in the van to come abreast of me.

He had old Murnaghan's hat and coat on him, and he was slumped back dozy in the driver's seat. The car humped and bumped over the rutted rocks in the lane but he was almost immobile, just like the real Murnaghan, as if trailing cows was something he did every day of his life.

He played it well.

He stopped the van and wound down the window when he was up to me, and I took my cue and went bouncing over to him.

'How many of them are up at the house?' he said.

'There's only two at our house,' I said. 'A man and a woman. But they both have guns and the woman has my sister who is four and my brother who is eight in the room to the right as you go in the hall and if anything happens . . .'

'Aye, so!' he said. He said it just like a real countryman. I suppose they get a lot of country-men in the police these days, there being precious little work left in the country.

'You mind out for yourself, love,' he said. 'Keep out of the way if any trouble starts. We'll be taking care of the rest.'

'There's others down below,' I said. 'Maybe four or five of them or maybe more, I don't know. And there is a man at the bridge.'

'He's taken care of already!' he said. 'Off you

go now. There is no call to be getting the two up there interested in our conversation.'

I wanted to say a whole lot of things. Did he know about the radio? Did he know they might try to call up the man at the bridge and then find he wasn't there and then . . . my mind was all fuzzed up, because I couldn't understand what was happening. Even if Mr Purdy the postman had picked up Mum's note, how come they had been so fast getting to us? The note couldn't have got into the Sergeant in Goatstown till near ten, with Mr Purdy on his round, and then it would have taken time to round up cows and lookalikes for Benjy and Mr Murnaghan and . . . and there wasn't time to dwell on that, because however they had worked it, they were *here* and in a minute there were going to be blow-ups or fighting or worse, with James and Katya trapped in the middle of it.

I belted after the van.

'You mustn't do *anything*,' I called in the window at him. 'D'you hear me? That woman has James and Katya and . . .'

'Leave it to us, and keep clear!' the big man grunted.

I didn't see what they could do. Just the two

of them ... unless the van was packed with a few more. How many could you get in a van like that? The back windows were painted over, so I couldn't see inside, but she was moving heavy. But then it *was* old Murnaghan's van, and Murnaghan's van never moves anything but heavy, being an antique.

I wanted to get it into their heads that there was no move at all they could make, while Paula Gettigan still had the two children to herself in our front room. The best they could do was to report back to whoever had sent them.

Then I thought ... *Mum!*

Would she catch on to it in time?

And there was my mum in the yard *Hiya Benjy-ing* the young one and chasing after the cows to keep off the tiles by the porch, the way she would anytime, and never a bleat of surprise out of her.

She was great.

She never turned a hair.

There she was introducing *Mr Murnaghan the man that owns all the cows* to our dear friend Paul Gettigan that had come up for a holiday with his wife all the way from Enniskillen, polite as you like.

The old man was clever. He'd taken on board the room the children were in, for he had the van pulled up next the house, in such a way that the back doors couldn't be seen from the window. He heaved out of the front seat, hands in his pockets and old pipe stuck in the corner of his mouth and it was *How-are-ye-the-day,-Eileen?* and *pleased-to-meet-you-Mr-Gettigan*, nattering away just like the real Mr Murnaghan would, and at the same time yelling his limpy way across the yard. He herded my mum and Paul Gettigan at the same time as he was herding the cows, managing things so they were carried along in front of him, away from the van and the porch.

A cow took a run at me, and the Benjy one took the chance to drop back and give a howl at it.

'Where's the radio?' he said.

'It is up in the barn,' I said. 'There is no way he can get up to it, without you seeing him. And my mum is clever enough to head him off. She won't let him near it!'

'Then we have him!' the young one said.

'The one at the bridge . . .' I said.

'We had him hours ago!' he said. 'Your man has been carrying on a conversation with *our* man, never knowing it!'

So they had taken out the man at the bridge. It must have been a policeman who had broadcast the warning up to the house, which seemed to me a bit of a risk. Then I thought . . . well, they couldn't get the men they needed on to the headland any other way but over the humpy bridge, so they had had to take him out. By the same token, they had to report the cows coming to the Gettigans if they were to retain the element of surprise and get up to the house. At least I thought something like that . . . I don't know whether I had worked it all out then. I was a muddle, full of all sorts of thoughts, because too much was going on for me to take it all in.

'There's no radio contact in the house?' he said.

'No,' I said, hoping I was right. Could Mrs Gettigan have some kind of handset on her? Would they have thought of that?

The old one had made a havers of the cows. They were milling round the yard, putting Paul Gettigan into a backwards-bolt at the far end of the yard, with the old one and my mother with him, while we were near the porch door.

'Can you call the children out of the room, away from her?' the young one asked, still doing his feinting at the cows, giving the impression that he was driving them, but really adding to the confusion.

'I don't know. There's no way I can do it that I can see. But you mustn't do a single thing until they *are* away from her.'

'It is a right tickler, that!' the Benjy one said, and then he headed off after the cows again. The other three had moved up by the gate, and my mum was taking the wire loop off the top for them to drive the cows through.

Paul Gettigan wasn't looking happy.

There was a big bullock that seemed to have a notion of him, and he was in retreat. When the gate was open, he went through into the field, but I didn't like the look of him. Any minute now, and he might realize that the whole cow business was a put-up show to separate him from his lady friend.

I thought *maybe it is me talking to the young one giving the game away*, so I went after the cows, up toward the gate, making for them. Mum was doing much better than I was. She was keeping a grip on herself, and chatting away to Murnaghan and Paul Gettigan as if she did it every day of her life.

Just the same, I was thinking, her heart must be in her boots.

Were there others in the van?

There had to be others.

You don't pull SAS-type raids single-handed.

That was my first thought.

Then I thought, maybe sometimes you have to.

For instance, if there is a woman sitting in a room ready to put a gun at the heads of two small children, an eight-year-old and a four-year-old.

It would be precious little good sending twenty or thirty big men in over the back wall of the field with their tear gas and their smoke bombs or whatever. That would be one sure way of winning the battle, but losing the war.

I'd seen enough of Paula Gettigan to know that she meant what she said. She wouldn't turn a hair of her dainty-dyed locks if she had to walk out of our house with the two children in front of her, ready to blow them to Kingdom Come if anybody tried to stop her.

Maybe it was just the two of them. The young one like Benjy, and the old one like Mr Murnaghan. Maybe they were kind of James Bonds with some wonder tricks up their sleeves, like you see in the films on TV.

Only it wasn't a film on TV.

It was happening here, out at the rocks of Dooney, at our old house with the cows and the hens and the bumpy lane and the broken-down bicycle as the props.

If it was two against two . . . well, it wasn't.

It was two against four, for Mum and I were involved as well.

Two against six, if you counted James and Katya, but of course they were too small to count. The thing about them that counted was that they were too small to know the danger they were in, and that overbalanced the calculation on everything else.

'I'm quare and dry!' 'Mr Murnaghan' said, spitting on the ground by his feet, and rubbing his hands together like an old countryman.

It was the cue for Mum to invite him into the house to meet Mrs Gettigan, which is where he wanted to go, obviously. Mum knew that, and I knew that, but the trouble was that Paul Gettigan had warned us about letting anyone into the house in advance.

'Well . . .' my mum said, looking hard at Gettigan.

She didn't know what to do. She was stuck.

If it had been the real Mr Murnaghan Mum would have had to invite him in. She couldn't turn round and say, *I'm very sorry Mr Murnaghan but you can't come in for a cup of tea because I am not allowed to let you over the doorstep for fear my children get shot.*

That is what my mum was telegraphing to Paul Gettigan. He would have to let us go in the house, or he would have to come up with something, for she couldn't.

It was a clever move of Mum's, it put the ball in his court.

I thought, *this is it.*

If we could get 'Mr Murnaghan' and 'Benjy' into the house, then surely they would be able to do something? They couldn't have planned anything out beforehand, because they had no way of knowing what they would find in our house before they got here. Well, now they knew. It was up to them, but it depended what way Paul Gettigan jumped.

Then I thought, *He's going to pull his gun now.*

Mum was the nearest one to him.

He was going to pull it on her. I could see the calculation flicker in his eyes. He was still hesitating when I waded in.

'I'll just nip into the house and put the kettle on, Mum,' I said.

I was staring straight at Paul Gettigan. He thought I was being smart, playing along with his orders. He nodded, and grinned at me, as if to say you've-learned-your-lesson-well-Ruth.

I breathed again. He thought I was doing what I was told, heading off trouble before it had got to the point where I knew he would have to take action.

'That's a good child!' our Mr Murnaghan said, turning to me. 'Mind you take care of the sugar lumps now.'

Was 'mind you take care of the sugar lumps' some kind of code message I was supposed to take up on? I suppose it was, but at the time I missed it.

I ran round the front of the house, and headed up to the porch.

The back door of the van was open, but the window of the room Mrs Gettigan had the children in was between the front of the van and the porch. If there were men in the van, could they have got into the house, past the window, without her seeing them?

Maybe there never was anybody in the van but the old man.

But the back doors of the van were *open*.

That meant . . . I was still working out what that meant when I passed through the door.

There was a soldier on the stairs in combat dress, his face streaked, pointing his gun straight at me.

I just froze.

He wagged the gun.

There was never a sound out of him.

I didn't speak to him either.

I thought, *I can't say a word to him, for she'll hear me*.

It was weird, a soldier like that with a gun, crouching on our stairs.

I made a stop sign at him, pushing back with both hands.

Then I pointed at the door into the front room, where she had the children. He wagged the gun again in acknowledgement and I made a 'NO' with my mouth, only I didn't say anything because I couldn't.

He nodded.

I went through the other door, into our kitchen.

There was a stir behind me, and something rammed hard against the back of my neck, and at the same moment a hand came down over my mouth and nose, and somebody pulled my head back. It was so sharp and sudden that I never had a chance to make any noise.

The soldier did it really well.

He kind of collapsed me onto the floor, backwards, slowly, all the time with the gun barrel against my neck.

Not a word.

Not a sound.

He was only young, in his twenties maybe. His face was all dirtied up with the black stuff, like the other one, and he had a big, thick, padded bullet-proof jacket on him, and a kind of visor thing down over his eyes, and the gun.

He must have seen who I was quick enough, for he pulled back the gun, and then he gave me a shushing sign with his lips, and removed his hand from my face.

His hand was all dirty, so I suppose my face was too.

The shushing sound meant he had it summed up. He knew she must be close to the door on the other side of the hallway, not four foot away, and she'd be listening for any give-away sound.

I made a sign at the open door I'd just come

through from the hall, indicating the other door, into the front room. The two doors are right opposite each other and terrible draughty, which is why we have the porch built on, but it isn't a bit of use.

He nodded, as if he understood.

I got up, thinking fast.

I made a sign at the soldier to hold still, and do nothing. I was wondering whether he would heed me, but he did.

I went over to the sink, singing out, 'I'm making a cup of tea for the men, Mrs Gettigan!'

There wasn't any reply from the room across the hall.

What was she doing in there?

I went over to the sink and filled the kettle and put it on the hob of the range, making sure I did it as noisily as I could, so that she would be sure to hear me. I was afraid that if she didn't hear that she would twig I was only acting, and that something had gone wrong.

As I pulled back from the sink, a soldier came in the window and crouched there, on top of the draining board, all in dead-dead-dead silence. I don't know how he did it. Just like a cat. His face was mucky too, and I remember being surprised at how white and shiny his teeth were, and how his eyes looked.

I went back into the hall again.

The soldier on the stairs couldn't have come in the front, so I suppose he must have come from the van and gone round the back and up our flat roof shed, and in the landing window. That way he couldn't be seen at all by Paula Gettigan if she'd tried taking a squint out the back window.

Silent soldiers everywhere, with their guns all ready to shoot ... and me in the middle of it, with the horrible feeling that I was the only one she *knew* to be there, and I had to do the talking. Our house was filling up with men and guns, and I was scared stiff that they would start using them.

I gave the one on the stairs the same no-no, keep back waggle with my hands. He nodded back and seemed to accept it.

I knocked on the door.

I was hoping she would open it.

They would be in on top of her if she did. They would have grenades and things, or smoke bombs, or something, and they'd chuck them and I would be in the middle trying to grab

Katya and James with bullets whizzing all around me.

'It's Ruth, Paula,' I called out. I thought I would give her the *Paula* so it would make her feel I was on her side, and then I realized it was a mistake, because I had never called her Paula yet, just 'you' or 'Mrs Gettigan'.

Well, if it was a mistake, I'd done it! There was no going back.

'Will you take a cup of tea, Paula?' I called. 'I'm making one for the men with the cows.'

'Stay clear of that door!'

That was all she said.

Had she realized what was going on, or was she just being cautious?

'It's all right,' I said. 'I'm making a drink for Mr Murnaghan and Benjy and when they have had it, they will clear off.'

Still no response.

I was left facing the closed door, afraid to touch it, so I went back into the kitchen.

Another soldier was coming through the window, which made three in the kitchen and one on the stairs.

One of them nodded toward the sink, as if he was telling me to move over there.

I did, and then he jerked his thumb silently, at the window.

Things had been happening out the back.

There is a kind of bank of grass beyond the window, sharply rising to the fence, and then the cow field, where I'd left the others.

There were two soldiers and a policeman up by the fence, bending over something on the ground.

All I could see of the something on the ground was a pair of yellow shoes.

One down, and one to go.

I turned away from the window. I was feeling sick inside. I didn't know if Paul Gettigan was dead or not. I didn't want him to be dead, but I didn't want any of our ones to be dead either.

The soldier behind the door gave me a thumbs up sign, and a grin of encouragement.

I had to think quickly, because I was the one who *knew* the situation, they had just come through a kitchen window into the middle of it. They would know where the rooms were, I suppose, because somebody would have shown them a room plan, but they couldn't know what was happening. I had to keep them away from the front room, in case the woman would take it out on James and Katya.

How to do it?

I was afraid even to whisper.

Katya's things!

She'd been paint-boxing with Paula Gettigan earlier on, and they were still laid out on the table. Her paints, and her crayons and a big sheet of painted-on paper, and Mrs Gettigan's sweetie bag. It was a big, big sweetie bag, thank goodness!

I got one of her felt tips, and started writing on the bag, then I held it up for them to see when I had finished.

THE WOMAN IS IN THE
NEXT ROOM.
SHE HAS A GUN.

My soldier, the one by the door who'd pulled me down, nodded.

I wrote some more.

SHE HAS MY BABY SISTER.

Anotner nod.

MY SISTER IS FOUR. MY BROTHER
IS EIGHT.
SHE HAS MY BROTHER TOO.

Then I was running out of bag! I was stuck
for a moment, then I just turned the bag over,
and wrote on the other side.

DON'T GO IN THERE

I wrote that in very big letters and underlined
the 'don't' three times.
My soldier nodded again.
Then he reached out and took the bag off me,
and the crayon.

CAN WE GET AT THEM?

Then he added.

DON'T WORRY!
IT WILL BE ALL RIGHT.

That was silly, about as silly as me giving the
children's ages. What help was that supposed to
be to anybody in the mess we were in?

DON'T KNOW!

I wrote on the back of Katya's painting . . . she wouldn't be pleased when she saw it . . . and I held it up, giving a hopeless shrug to back it.

We stood there looking at each other.

The three other soldiers . . . or was it four, I don't know, I can't remember rightly . . . the other soldiers crowded in the room were just like statues. I don't know how they did it. I couldn't even see them breathe. I was thinking how strange it was to be standing, playing crayon-writing-games and miming things, with armed soldiers in the room, and my brother and sister trapped with a gun lady in the room next door. Real, but it wasn't real. It *couldn't* be happening.

But of course it was.

My mind was going sixteen to the dozen.

Paula Gettigan was cute. She wouldn't budge out of there until she thought the coast was clear, and she wouldn't believe that until she saw the van go off. Even then she would probably wait until Paul Gettigan came to her before she opened the door. She wasn't going to leave the room without James and Katya. But, Paul Gettigan wouldn't be able to go to her, for they had him laid out on the ground behind the kitchen window with a gun in his neck, which was a big mistake, really. They shouldn't have jumped him until they had made certain of the children ... but then maybe there had been no alternative. He must have panicked and gone for his gun, and that would have been that.

'Ruth?'

She was calling me, through the closed door.

I looked at my soldier.

He nodded.

'Yes, Mrs Gettigan?' I said, going out into the hall. I didn't make the calling-her-Paula mistake a second time. We weren't really on first name terms.

'I have Katya here where I need her, Ruth,' Mrs Gettigan called through the door.

'Yes,' I said.

'I want you in here too, Ruth,' she said.

Pause, while my heart missed a beat.

'Tell them to stay clear, Ruth,' she said, very slowly and distinctly, so that there could be no mistake about it.

She *knew*! Maybe she had seen something through the window, or heard something. Maybe she had spotted one of them in the yard. Anyway, she knew.

'You are to open the door yourself, Ruth, and come through it alone.' Then she added, 'Katya wants you to open the door.'

That was just to remind me.

I opened the door.

She was crouched against the side of the piano, on the far side of the room, where it made a shield for her against anyone who might try to spot her from the front window. She had Katya held in front of her, and James by her side . . . the other side, blocking the line of fire from the back window.

She was shielded in both directions.

She had the gun held to James' head. It was James she was going to shoot if anyone tried to jump her.

She didn't move when I opened the door.

There wasn't a quiver or a quake in her. In her shoes, I would have been all over the floor, but she had every nerve laced up, every hair in place. Small, and fair and pretty, with the gun firm in her fist.

'Tell them to get out of the house, Ruth,' she said. Then she did it for me. 'Get out! GET OUT!' she yelled.

'Do what she says!' I said, over my shoulder. 'You have to, for she has my wee brother and she'll kill him.'

They were good.

The three or four in the kitchen came out, and went down the hall, out the front, making sure she could see them. The one on the side of me nearest the front door, the one who'd been crouching in the porch, went too. That left the one on the stairs. He didn't move.

What could I do?

I couldn't say to him to go, because he might misunderstand me and burst down the stairs shooting. He couldn't see what was in the room. I suppose he thought he would be able to shoot her as she came out the door. He couldn't see what I could see, that she had the gun tight against James' neck. Even if the soldier killed her, she would still kill James.

'Are they gone?' she demanded. 'All gone?'

I looked at James and Katya.

They stared back at me.

Katya was crying, softly. James was dead pale and frightened, poor little thing.

Neither of them said a word, but I think James understood. I can't think what must have been going on in Katya's wee head.

'No,' I said, taking a deep breath. 'They are not gone. There is one up above me on the stairs, with a gun.'

It wasn't very brave of me, but I had to do it. There was nothing else I could do. She had James and Katya, and she had the gun pressed into James' neck, pushing down his shirt collar, and that was it.

'Go, you!' I yelled at the soldier.

He came down the stairs past me, glancing in the room, but she was smart enough. From where he was, in the hall, I doubt if he could have seen her well enough to get in a shot, without killing Katya.

'Close the door,' she said.

I was just in the room by this time, her side of the door. I closed it behind me.

'How many of them?' she said, still crouching by the piano, right across the room from me, so I couldn't make any move to get at her. I don't think I would have managed it anyway . . . not without her shooting James first.

'I've seen about six of them,' I said. 'But there are probably more.'

'What's happened down at the bungalow?'

'I don't know,' I said. Then I added, 'They got the one who was guarding the bridge ages ago, that is how they have so many here now.' It wasn't much of a hope, but I had the feeling that if I was straight and honest with her it would make more sense than trying to lie. Anyway, the worse she thought it was, the more chance there might be that she would give up.

'Don't come any closer,' she said, shoving the gun harder into James' neck.

'They have Paul already,' I said. 'They'll get the other ones down below. I don't think you can do anything. I think you should give in.'

She never batted an eyelid. She wasn't giving in.

I had to think of something to say that would make some difference, so I lied in my teeth again.

'You don't seem so bad to me,' I said. 'You are not a psycho whatever it is, like some, are you? And you're not going to get away with it. They'll shoot you as you come out of the door.'

'Not with Katya and James,' she said. 'And you, Ruth.'

'But . . .'

'You go over and open that window and you tell them what the score is,' she said. 'Tell them I want nobody, but *nobody*, around the yard and I want our van by the door. Tell them I'm not going to talk or bargain or do anything but get into that van and go and if they try anything the blood won't be on my hands.'

I did what I was told.

The policeman who had been acting that he was Mr Murnaghan started answering back, but she would have none of it.

'I'm not talking to anybody,' she said. 'Men in the yard or not, I'm coming out *now*, and I'm coming out with Katya in front of me and a gun at James' head and if I get shot, James gets shot. Tell them that.'

I told them.

'And we're coming now!' she yelled from the back of the room.

Then she got up and started for the door, sideways walking like a crab, from the effort of keeping hold of Katya and James at the same time. She lifted Katya up in one arm, and kept the gun pressed into James with the other. The hand of the arm that was holding Katya gripped James by the shoulder, so he couldn't do a quick move. Not that he could have. He was petrified, poor little thing.

I was thinking *Well, that is your arms full, anyway.* Maybe if I could get alongside her I could throw her away from James, off balance.

'Is the van there?' she said.

'No,' I said.

'Then we'll go to it,' she said.

I just nodded.

'You go first, Ruth,' she said, 'Well in front of me. You go out and you go over to the van. Then you take a look to see that they haven't fixed it someway, drained off the petrol or anything like that. Then you come back in here and tell me. And if you do one thing different to that James gets shot, and I still have Katya, so see you don't.'

I did as I was told again.

The yard was clear. I don't know where they were. I suppose they were in the field. I thought there might have been one of them crouching by the wheels, or tucked up in the back of the van, but there wasn't, and that was a relief, because I had made up my mind that I was going to tell her if there was anybody. So long as she had the gun at James' neck there was nothing else I could do.

I couldn't see that they would have had time to booby trap it or anything, and anyway a booby trap would have meant us going up in smoke as well, which didn't make good sense.

It was odd. I didn't know Paula Gettigan at all, and yet here I was caught up with her in what might be the end of my life.

I went back into the house, and into the room. She hadn't moved.

'It looks all right to me,' I said. 'But I'm no hand at vans. I wouldn't know if it wasn't.'

'It is a risk we'll have to take together!' she said.

'You don't have to take it,' I said, despairingly. 'You could give up.'

'I'm not giving up, and I'm not staying here till they talk me out of it,' she said. She'd seen all the siege films too. I suppose something like that was in her mind. That was why she had decided to go at once, right at the beginning, before they had time to set traps for her.

'You first,' she said. 'I'll be a step or two behind you with the children.'

I did what I was told again.

She came out on the porch behind me, carefully looking round.

There was a big plume of smoke rising from the bungalow. It was on fire then, though I didn't know how much on fire it was, until later. The other half of the operation had already swung into action. They had gone into the bungalow below with no holds barred.

'Do you drive?' she said, standing in the yard.

'No,' I said. 'I'm fourteen. No licence.' Of course that wasn't what she meant. Round the country lots of kids drive, but anyway I don't.

'Well, go over and walk round the van again, and if there is anyone there, get them away,' she said.

I did, and there wasn't.

'All right,' I said.

She came across the yard, awkwardly, because of trying to hold Katya up in front of her as a shield and keep a grip on James, with the gun against his neck at the same time.

If they shot her, she would shoot him.

Simple.

I came round, and pulled open the nearside

door for her, because she hadn't a free hand to open it with.

'In you go, James,' she said.

James clambered in.

She steadied herself, to lower herself in after him and, just for a moment, she had the gun in the air, away from James' neck, her gun hand resting on the roof of the van.

James was half-turned, looking at her.

He did the most incredible thing!

I don't think he had time to think about what he was doing. It must have been half fear, half animal instinct, and the third half . . . that makes one and a half . . . self-preservation.

He bit her.

There was her arm, flesh exposed, up above his face. She had one foot already in the van, with her weight and Katya's weight falling full on the other one, which was on the ground where it would be, just beside the van.

And James turned his head and reached up and sank his teeth in her arm.

And I hit her.

I don't know what I hit her with . . . just me, and there's a lot of me, a sort of wild bull dive right into her gut. She went over with me on top of her. I was kicking and punching at her and pulling Katya and we were down in a bundle on the ground and rolling about in the dust.

And then it was over.

I don't know where they came from.

James says two of the soldiers came off the roof of the house behind us. But there were others as well, coming from every direction, arriving all together, soldiers and policemen.

It didn't matter.

The next thing I knew was that the big young one, the Benjy one, was holding onto me and I was crying and sobbing. There were bleeding scrapes on me where she had gone at my face with her nails. My mum was down in the yard on her knees hugging Katya and James both at once, with them clinging to her and crying and she just rocking them and telling them, 'It is all right. It is all right.'

And it was.

It shouldn't have been, but it was.

Chapter 11

Well, that is it, really. That is what happened to us out on the rocks of Dooney, where no one ever comes.

There is nothing more left to tell.

It was a horrible time. The worst time ever in my life, I hope. I hope I never have a worse one, and I can't think what a worse one would be.

If that is what living dangerously is like, then I want no part of it, and neither does anybody else in my family. There was no nice Uncle Bill to rescue everybody, and no parrot, and no clues on parchments or secret tunnels.

Just us, and the old rocks, and a man and a woman who might have killed us.

They are all arrested and put away now. Well, the Gettigans anyway, though they were only unimportant ones, and the ones at the bungalow below. The police didn't get the ones in the boat, who were to come in to our harbour and move the stuff after it was dug out of the old bungalow floor. If the boat had come when it was supposed to, they might all have got away. The stuff they were after was the leftover of some bullion raid down in the midlands, across the border in the Republic. It was very heavy stuff, in boxes, and they'd stashed it in the bungalow under the new floor they had put in for the purpose. The idea was to let the hunt for it get cold, and then to move it on years later, when nobody would be left looking out for it. There was billions of it apparently . . . well, a whole lot of gold bars, the kind of money that makes you lose count.

The police said that they didn't think we were meant to be used as hostages, if the thing had worked out right. The bullion people didn't know about us until the wet-man's visit . . . they'd purposely kept away from where they had the bullion hidden . . . and it must have been a shock to them to find us sitting just where they didn't want us to be. They were faced with the fact that they couldn't dig up the bungalow floor and load all those heavy boxes on their boat without our noticing what was going on, and they were afraid we might have talked about it.

That's how our strange visitors came. If it had all worked out, we would have been tied up in the house while the Gettigans went abroad with the boat . . . they would have been the only ones we could identify. That would have been that.

What they didn't know, was that they were under police surveillance anyway! They hadn't been arrested, because that wouldn't have got the banks and insurance companies their money back. The police had no idea where the bullion was, and couldn't have, until the time came for it to be moved.

But the Maguires got in the way.

I think that is the interesting bit.

It started off about *money*, whether the bullion people could find a safe place to hide it, and whether they would get away with it, or whether the police would get it back.

By the end, it wasn't about money at all. It was about whether we would come out of the whole thing alive.

We did, but it wasn't thanks to all my working things out, and schemes for getting help. It was down to one mad minute, and James' sharp teeth. He didn't *think* that out, there wasn't time, he just did it.

Mum was the one who did the thinking, she was the real heroine. If she had put one foot wrong we might not have made it, but she didn't.

She concentrated her whole mind on saving James and Katya and me, nothing else.

I suppose I would like to have been a heroine, doing something clever and brilliant and brave and saving everybody's bacon, like the girl detectives in James' stories, but when it came to living through the real experience it wasn't like that. I didn't feel brave or brilliant at all, just scared.

I survived, that's what I did!

I came through it with nothing but a bad shaking and a few cuts and bruises from my scramble down the Black Rock Gully and my tumble in the yard with Mrs Gettigan.

We *all* survived.

That's good enough for me.

WAR BOY
Michael Foreman

Barbed wire and barrage ballons, gas masks and Anderson shelters, loud bangs and piercing whines – the sights and sounds of war were all too familiar to a young boy growing up in the 1940s.

But gas masks were great for rude noises, gobstoppers were still good to suck and the Hill Green Gang could still try to beat the Ship Road Gang. Father Christmas would tell tales of his days as a cabin boy on the great clippers, the old tramp could spin a good yarn round the camp fire, and nothing could beat Mrs Ruthern's rabbit pie!

OUR KID
Ann Pilling

Frank has high hopes that the money from his paper round will solve all his problems, but the new job plunges him into another world. He meets Tim, with his rich family and his gorgeous sister Cass, and Sister Maggie at the convent (why, he wonders, do nuns read the *TV Times*?) then there's Foxy, hanging about the streets at all hours.

Frank emerges from this warm and fascinating novel with a new view of his slob of a big brother, his lonely dad, and Foxy, the cat burglar, and discovers 'the amazing things people will do for love.'

THE SPELL SINGER AND OTHER STORIES
ed. Beverley Mathias

The lively, enterprising children in these stories all have some form of disability, and they also have some marvellous adventures. One foils a handbag snatch, another struggles to save the life of a woodpigeon, one learns to swim with seals in the sea, and one helps solve a bank robbery.

Including writers as varied as Joan Aiken, Vivien Alcock, Allan Baillie, Michael Morpurgo and Geraldine Kaye, this is a hugely enjoyable collection of stories. It is published in association with The National Library for the Handicapped Child.

RT, MARGARET AND THE RATS OF NIMH
June Leslie Conly

When Margaret and her brother RT get lost in the forests surrounding Thorn Valley, help comes from an unexpected quarter when the super-rats of NIMH come to their rescue. Margaret and RT must return home before winter sets in, but the incredible events of their summer in the valley become the biggest secret they have ever had to keep.

The third thrilling story in this classic trilogy about the rats of NIMH.

ONLY MIRANDA
Tessa Krailing

A new town, a tiny flat over the Chinese takeaway, a new school mid-term and a place next to Chrissie Simpson, the most unpopular girl in the class. Things aren't looking great for Miranda. But her father has gone to prison and this at least is a chance of a new life for her and her mother. Miranda bounces back in true style: she befriends poor Chrissie and when the dinner money is stolen and Chrissie is suspected, Miranda is determined to prove her innocence.

TWIN AND SUPER TWIN
Gillian Cross

Ben, David and Mitch had only meant to start the Wellington Street Gang's bonfire, not blow up all their fireworks as well. But even worse is what happens to David's arm in the process. Until, that is, they realize that this extraordinary event could be very useful in their battles with the Wellington Street Gang.